The Old Child

JENNY ERPENBECK was born in East Berlin in 1967. She learned bookbinding, studied theatre sciences and worked backstage at the Staatsoper theatre in Berlin before becoming an opera director and writer. She has now published a play and a collection of short stories. Her fiction has been translated worldwide and *The Old Child* was awarded one of Germany's Aspekte Prizes for Literature.

SUSAN BERNOFSKY has translated works by Robert Walser, Hermann Hesse, Gregor von Rezzori, Yoko Tawada, Ludwig Harig and Peter Szondi. She is the author of *Foreign Words: Translator-Authors in the Age of Goethe* and is currently at work on a biography of Robert Walser. Her translation of *The Old Child and Other Stories* was awarded the Helen and Kurt Wolff Prize 2006.

From the reviews of The Old Child:

'Although the prettily packaged exterior suggests something sweet, there's darkness at the heart of *The Old Child*... It's an unsettling tale and the twist in its conclusion makes the idea of adopting antisocial behaviour to avoid engaging with real life even more discomforting... The creeping feeling of unease that permeates the novella is exacerbated by the pared-down poetics of the writing, which is at once lyrical and astringent.' *Metro*
****

'This taut and troubling tale has a wider resonance. The girl stands in a long line of German literary protagonists traumatized into inarticulacy, forgetfulness or arrested development... When this bleakly compelling novella was published, Erpenbeck was hailed as one of the most striking and original new voices in German writing. Susan Bernofsky's translation powerfully conveys the rhythm and tone of Erpenbeck's dry, laconic prose.' *Independent*

'Oppressive, charming, scary... Jenny Erpenbeck is the rising star of the German literary scene.' *Cosmopolitan*

'Jenny Erpenbeck's literary magic is in her X-ray vision. Wherever her sharp gaze falls, things change in a flash, the surface melts away, and there appears beneath it her character's motivation... Sensational.' *Frankfurter Allgemeine Zeitung*

'Erpenbeck will get under your skin.' *Washington Post*

'Writing so concentrated, so dense, that a slim volume packs the weight of the world.' *Hamburger Morgenpost*

From the reviews of The Book of Words:

'An exceedingly well-crafted story, that makes for an unsettling realization—and for a book that is neither easily digested nor easily forgotten.' *The Times*

'Ambitious in technique and scope, *The Book of Words* reaches at times into the realm of magical realism... The construction is intricate and masterly. Seemingly innocent words for seemingly innocent things one by one ambush the reader with their true meaning as the narrative moves towards its horrific denouement. Masterly.' *Independent*

'A sinisterly lyrical novel... its lack of emotional flamboyance gives its climax the quality of an avalanche.' *The Believer*

'The whole thing might be a novel by Lizzie Borden told in the spiky recalcitrant voice of Angela Carter.' *Scotland on Sunday*

The Old Child

and

The Book of Words

Jenny Erpenbeck

Translated from the German
by Susan Bernofsky

BOOKS

First published by Portobello Books Ltd in 2006 and 2007
This omnibus paperback edition published in 2008

Portobello Books Ltd
Twelve Addison Avenue
Holland Park
London W11 4QR

Copyright © Jenny Erpenbeck 1999 and 2005
Translation © Susan Bernofsky 2005 and 2007

The Old Child was first published in the original German
by Eichborn Verlag AG, Frankfurt am Main as Geschichte vom alten
Kind in 1999. English translation was first published simultaneously by
New Directions in the USA and by Penguin Books Canada in The
Old Child & Other Stories in 2005. The Book of Words was first
published in the original German by Eichborn Verlag AG,
Frankfurt am Main as Wörterbuch in 2005.

The right of Jenny Erpenbeck to be identified as the author of
this work and Susan Bernofsky's right to be identified as its translator
have been asserted by them in accordance with the Copyright,
Designs and Patents Act 1988.

The publication of this work was supported by grants from
the Goethe-Institut and the Arts Council.

This is a work of fiction. The characters, incidents, and
dialogues are products of the author's imagination and not to
be construed as real. The author's use of names of actual persons,
living or dead, and actual places is incidental to the purposes of
the plot and is not intended to change the entirely fictional
character of the work.

A CIP catalogue record is available from the British Library

2 4 6 8 9 7 5 3 1

ISBN 978 1 84627 058 1

www.portobellobooks.com

Designed and typeset in Poliphilus by Patty Rennie

Printed in Great Britain by CPI Bookmarque, Croydon

The Old Child

For my mother

When they found her, she was standing on the street with an empty bucket in one hand, on a street lined with shops, and didn't say a word. When she was brought to the police station, all the official questions were put to her: What her name was, where she lived, her parents, her age. The girl replied that she was fourteen years old, but she couldn't tell them her name, nor where her home was. At first, the policemen had called the girl "miss", but now they stopped. They said: How can you not know where you came from, where you were before you stood on the street here with your empty bucket? The girl simply could not remember, she couldn't remember the beginning. She was an orphan through and through, and all she had, all she knew was the empty bucket she held in one hand and continued to hold as the policemen questioned her. One of the men tried to insult the girl, saying: Scraping the bottom of the bucket, eh? But the girl didn't even notice that his words were meant to give offense, she replied simply: Yes.

The official inquiries produced no further information. The girl was indisputably present in all her height and bulk, but as for her origins and history, she was so surrounded by nothingness that there seemed, from the beginning, to be something implausible about her very existence. So they relieved her of her bucket, took her by her fleshy hand, and brought her to the Home for Children.

The girl has a wide, blotchy face that looks like a moon with shadows on it, she has broad shoulders like a swimmer's, and from the shoulders downward she appears to have been hewn from a single block of wood, there is neither a swelling where the breasts should be, nor an indentation at the waist. The legs are sturdy, the hands as well, and nonetheless the girl does not make a convincing impression, perhaps because of her hair. This hair is neither long nor short, it forms a fringe at the nape of the neck and is neither brown nor genuinely black—it is at most as black as the cloth of a flag that has been hanging too long in the sun and is bleached out, there are moments when it appears nearly gray. The girl moves slowly, and if she should happen not to move slowly, little beads of sweat appear on the bridge of her nose. The girl knows she is bigger than she should be, and so she hunches her shoulders and keeps her head down. She hunches as though she were obliged to do so, to hold back a great force that is raging inside her.

The Home where the police have deposited the girl is the largest in this city. It is located in the city's most outlying district, the district that borders the woods, and is comprised of several buildings distributed across the extensive, meandering grounds. There are living quarters, a nursery school, a school for the lower and one for the upper classes, as well as a kitchen building, a gymnasium, an assembly hall, a quadrangle paved in concrete, a soccer field, and outbuildings in which various workshops are housed—here the pupils are to learn to work hard, just as Life will one day require of them. Surrounding all this there is a fence, a fence with a single gate at which a guard is posted, one has to speak with him to enter the Home or leave it. Through this gate, the down-at-heels or prosperous parents come to visit on weekends, weeping parents and parents who do not weep, but for some of the children, neither down-at-heels, nor prosperous, nor weeping, nor any other sort of parents pass through this gate. The gate also admits strangers who wish to become parents, they come here to have a look at the children, but for some children even strangers do not come. There are children that are so unclean, so massive or coarse that they need not even be rejected: no one looks at them to begin with, they cannot pass through the screen that has been woven to aid in these selections. They are here, but no one sees them. The girl will doubtless be one of these. And yet her invisibility appears to be something even more fundamental: the entire figure of the girl is so askew— even her way of walking is askew—that if you wanted to take her by the hand it would be like thrusting your hand into emptiness.

On this still-warm day in autumn, then, the girl can walk across the thin grass of the sports field without the least agitation, despite all the parents, or those who wish to become parents, seated on the wooden rails that frame the field. For while these parents and would-be parents keep their eyes fixed on the field, observing their children, or the children who will one day be theirs, engaged in various activities, they do not take note of the girl, it is as if she were impervious to their glances. None of these down-at-heels and weeping and other sorts of parents, nor any of the strangers who wish to become parents will see her walking across the field. That's just the way she's planned it. Just as others strive to break out of fenced-in enclosures, to escape from prison, the workhouse, the insane asylum or barracks, the girl has achieved quite the opposite: she has broken into such an enclosure, the Home for Children to be precise, and it is highly unlikely that anyone would think of taking her back out through the gate, thrusting her back into the world.

And so she walks across the field with utter calm, gnawing as she goes upon her fingernail. And when on her very first day one of the littlest boys bumps into her as she is walking across the field with her nail between her lips, bumps her so that she almost falls down and has to catch herself with one hand, she begins to sob for one brief moment, but this she finds not unpleasurable. For the circumstance that a little boy has bumped her to make her fall in the mud, indeed has bumped her so hard she has to sob, awakens in the girl the hope that she will be permitted to occupy one of the lower rungs in the school's hierarchy, perhaps even the lowermost one, and the lowermost place is always the safest, it is the one whose requirements she will most definitely be able to live up to. And so she doesn't even wipe the mud from her hand, but instead continues to walk, still sobbing just a little, and then goes back to gnawing her fingernail, which now is dirty.

When they first brought her to her room, which is above all a room for sleeping, to be shared with three other girls, it was one of the happiest moments of her life. This room was free of disorder of any sort, it contained four beds, each placed against one of the four walls, and all four of them neatly made up, and beside each one a chair and a metal locker. The locker is meant to hold the week's bundle of clothes, as well as the books for school and notebooks, and the few personal items a child might collect or, if it has saved enough, buy with its pocket money. To be sure, the economical child is as likely as not to find these items stolen. As a matter of principle, the lockers have no locks. A communal spirit is to be fostered. All the items a child brings with it when it enters the Home are confiscated and then discarded, for its arrival here constitutes a New Beginning.

At this time of day, none of the other girls is in the room, because it is not yet bedtime and entering the room before bedtime is not permitted. It isn't a room for daytime activities. The instructress speaks, the girl listens and nods, she is allowed to peer briefly into her locker, in which everything is already arranged just as will be expected from now on. For a moment she thinks of her bucket, which always made a sound like someone sighing when it swung back and forth. Then she is told to take off everything she is wearing. She sits down on the edge of the bed and begins to pull off her trousers, then the stockings she is wearing beneath them, of good quality but full of holes, and she crosses her arms above her head to free herself from her matted woolen sweater, which is much too tight. Just imagine, she crosses her arms above her head for this, like a woman. The girl undresses down to a grayish camisole and grayish panties, then she gets up and trots after the instructress, who has gestured for her to follow. The instructress walks across the linoleum of the windowless hallway to the washroom, the girl behind her. In the wash-room she then surrenders her camisole and steps out of her panties, balancing on one leg at a time, ducking her head and glancing up at the instructress who is standing beside her, observing this obligatory transformation. The instructress has placed the girl's other things over her arm, and to these she now adds the camisole and panties. Now that she is naked, the girl looks very much like a block of wood. She gets up and steps into the shower. She begins to wash herself. Finally she is able to wash off the dirt covering her entire body, dirt such as collects on a body over time.

After the girl has washed, the instructress gives her the packet of clothes for the week. This clothing is issued by the laundry staff, all of the things are second, third and fourth hand, but they have been washed and are the right size for the recipient of the package. The girl slips into this clothing that has been assigned to her. While a number will be sewn into the sweaters, pants and skirts indicating that they will now belong to the girl until she outgrows them, the underpants and under-shirts as well as the nightgowns count as "linens", which means that once a week each child receives one pair of under-pants, one undershirt and one nightgown as part of the general laundry distribution, the underwear is, as it were, intended to clothe a single collective body, and anyone who is unhappy with this arrangement will be addressed as madame, and her protest will bear no fruit. But there is no need to address the girl as madame, she finds nothing to object to in this procedure and is moreover familiar with the charming admonition "No false delicacy!" of which this laundry arrangement reminds her. In any case, the collective under-pants restore to order something that had been threatened by disorder, that's what it feels like to the girl.

When she has then attained this condition, clad in the same standard-issue clothes as all the others here, and clean to precisely the same extent as all the others, she goes looking for a mirror. She wants to see what she looks like in this new life of hers, wants to see whether her face has changed with the advent of this New Life, but as she discovers, her new room has no mirror. She will wander about and notice that neither in the bathrooms nor in any of the halls, nor anywhere else in the Home has a mirror been provided. Finally she will ask, already anticipating the first twinges of a guilty conscience, and therefore as casually as possible, whether there is a mirror, and she will learn that vanity is one of the seven deadly sins, madame. And while the reproach contained in this answer demonstrates that the instructress is utterly blind to the nature of the causes that lead the girl to look for a mirror and, indeed, to eventually ask for one, her response illumines the principle that governs this fenced-in institution, and the girl knows no happier state than what she experiences when gazing upon the architecture of a principle. She knows no brighter, more beautiful sight.

The girl remembers the time of mirrors, when she noticed, at first with unease, then with interest and finally with satisfaction, indeed even a sort of pride, that her face had looked utterly unchanged for quite a long time, as if its round, fleshy form were repelling age. The girl had then begun to experiment with this unchangingness. For example, when an occasion for weeping presented itself, she would take advantage of this occasion to weep profusely and when she was done weeping would quickly go look at herself in the mirror. And behold, neither had her cheeks gone hollow with the exertion of her weeping, nor had her skin become porous, nor had shadows come to encircle her eyes. So she could weep as much as she liked and nonetheless be quite certain that this weeping would leave no traces behind on her large face. Another time, she lied to someone and checked in a mirror to see whether her face had been transformed into the face of a liar, but either her face had been from the beginning a liar's face or it simply had not changed as a result of the lie, though before the lie it hadn't been a liar's face and afterward, while it remained the same, it was the face of a liar. Even the time someone had unexpect-edly given her a very beautiful leather wallet stamped with the Leaning Tower of Pisa, she looked in the mirror, but the pleasure could not be distinguished in her features. Observing the constancy of her face, which is what made the girl acquire the habit of frequently looking in the mirror, hardly counts as vanity, but now the view that vanity was one of the seven deadly sins had been invoked to justify why it was not possi-ble to view one's own reflection anywhere in the Home, and the girl noted with gratitude that to her, as to all the others, one and the same set of reasons was being applied for encouraging one thing and discouraging another. Liberated from the task of monitoring her face, indeed forgetting it outright, the girl steps into the bright architecture of the principle upon which she has briefly been permitted to gaze.

When she came into the classroom and all the others were standing beside their desks and she herself was standing beside the teacher in front of them, she felt like Gulliver among the Lilliputians. She looked around her and saw that she could look down at all the other heads. That's when she realized she was too tall. She hunched her shoulders and waited for the teacher to assign her a seat. The teacher placed her in the one unoccupied seat, next to a boy with a rough-hewn face. That way the contrast wasn't so great, and the others were able to recover from their alarm and begin to believe that this was the new girl. The girls saw at a glance that the new girl was not a beauty who might disrupt their fine-spun hierarchy—for the moment such ponderous crea-tures sit down, they at once sink, a leaden sediment, to the depths of every hierarchy—and the boys knew they had landed a fine catch, sustenance for many a good laugh had just strolled right into their mouths, and this filled them with glee. From the smiling silence on the part of her classmates after she's been assigned her seat, the girl ventures to conclude that her awkwardness apparently suffices to secure her a place in this eighth-grade class, perhaps even the lowermost one, and at this she is relieved. At just this moment, a door can be heard shutting faintly somewhere, and it seems to the girl as if her old life has now departed from her.

The lesson proceeds, but the girl sits in silence, and the leaden script imprinted on her brain now tumbles into the blue sky outside the classroom windows, she surrenders each of her words and each of her thoughts until in the end she is left sitting there in a state of perfect emptiness, and one might well be moved to say of her: She is a blank slate.

This overgrown child begins to follow lessons, for example an eighth-grade lesson in mathematics: If x equals y, the straight line rises at a forty-five-degree angle. The girl listens to what is being said and to what is being thought, she listens to everything that is said and thought during an eighth-grade mathematics lesson. Somewhere she has already made the acquaintance of this straight line rising at its angle of forty-five degrees, and nonetheless she is astonished to meet it again on this side of the diagram. Something or other must be reversed, like a mirror image, or must once have been so. It seems to the girl as if she must have switched sides at some point, but when this was she cannot say. Headfirst through the looking glass.

The girl picks up her pen and awaits the arrival of the text. She doesn't have to wait long. The letters bend mutely to the left as if encountering some invisible resistance, the "n"s rehoist their flattened hillocks, the double underlines, executed with the aid of a ruler, present themselves contentedly for inspection. A lost age makes its entrance on a carpet of blue ink. The teacher picks up the notebook by the ears and says: Now you've got it.

On this side of the diagram it is customary to raise one's hand when one has something to say. One may then be permitted to speak, at the teacher's discretion. The mathematics teacher wants to go easy on the girl during the first lesson, to give her time to adjust, but when near the end of the hour her thick arm slowly rises above her head, he gives her a sign permitting her to speak. For the first time the girl speaks in her new circle of companions, she gives the answer to a simple question the teacher has asked, and her answer is wrong. Never mind, the teacher says, and gives the girl a particularly warm smile, since she has dared to speak for the first time, with so soft, thin and sweet a voice, a little sister of a voice, one that seems made for giving the wrong answer in the most pitiful way. That she meant to give the wrong answer, however, that she more or less stole it from her classmates, is a possibility that occurs to no one, all that can be sensed is a certain fakeness to her way of speaking, but since everyone steals in class as best he can, since everyone's eyes are directed deceptively and with faked attentiveness toward the front of the room, toward the teacher, this girlish little voice is received with a grin, and the lesson proceeds.

There must have been a time when the girl, too, thought of a bad grade as something bad, but this time is long past. Meanwhile she has learned that school is the place where errors must occur so as to give it meaning, school is the place of correction, and no bad grade has any real consequences, grades are utterly removed from reality, they stand for the contents of a head, something invisible. And when the teachers then insist that learning is something one does not for school but for Life, this serves only to reinforce the girl's faith that school and Life are two separate things. All that can happen to her here if such occurrences become too frequent is that the teacher will eventually give up on her, he will be unable to help noticing that the girl's capacity to forget is greater than her capacity to store in her head the subject matter of an eighth-grade class—mathematics, for instance—which would allow her and her head to advance to a ninth-grade classroom at the appointed time. And while the prospect of not being allowed to pass to the next grade might fill the others with terror, implying as it does an additional year of captivity, for the girl it would be a coup. Just as she gives the subject matter its freedom back by forgetting it, she, too, would like to gain her freedom by having the teachers say: This one you can forget about. What a blessing it must be to be given up on. What a blessing to gaze upon the backs of one's fellow students who are working their way forward amid the sweat and cold because for them, whether they like it or not, school and Life appear to form a single continuum. What a blessing to be able to observe their toils with a peace-filled heart. And while it would appear to be actual stupidity, stupidity almost even greater than that of a pupil occupying the lowermost rung in the hierarchy, that accounts for the girl's having been given up on by teachers and pupils alike—for clearly she is neither lazy, nor does she refuse to perform out of ill will, nor does she think she is better than the others, no, she is simply stupid—even having been given up on is not enough to sever her sense of belonging among the others, who unlike her are expending great effort to drive their minds along in front of them. Even the pace at which she walks causes the others' successes to stand out in their full significance, and it isn't out of laziness or ill will that she walks so far behind them, nor because she thinks she is better than they are, but rather for the simple reason that she can go no faster, for, the moment she takes as many as three steps, beads of sweat appear on the bridge of her nose, indicating that she has reached her limit. And precisely because she has been given up on, and because the girl gives no one cause for envy or a struggle, you can laugh at her, you can even shove her so that she nearly falls down, for no other reason than the delight you feel at the way the girl's very presence demonstrates the antithesis between those who get somewhere in life and this girl who is simply too stupid to get anywhere. And since the girl herself is equally grateful for this antithesis, or even more so, just from a different perspective, she feels at the moment when she is being given a shove that nearly makes her fall down, a moment when she might perhaps even sob a little, a great sense of relief at occupying this lowermost place that no one will fight her for, a place that does not require extreme expenditures of effort to attain and hold, all that is needed is a meticulous forgetfulness and the meticulous stupidity that results from it, as well as letting herself be shoved and sobbing a little. While the others no doubt know what is owed to them by Life: Life owes them freedom, and freedom lies outside the walls of this institution, the girl knows that in truth freedom is this: Not having to shove anyone yourself, and this freedom exists inside the walls of the institution and nowhere else. And if she simply allows herself to be shoved, she will keep her place in the institution forever and will never have to get anywhere, not even ninth grade.

For example it may happen that the girl is sitting in German class and the teacher is asking the children about *Puntila*, which they were to have read, the play *Puntila and His Man Matti*, by Bertolt Brecht. The teacher is a young woman with bleached-blond hair, about whom the rumor is circulating among the students that after school she frequents the tin shacks of the construction workers. Now and again she mentions a gentleman acquaintance, and now and again she appears in class in the morning with red eyes. Chronic conjunctivitis, she says. Now she has asked the children about *Puntila*, whereupon the girl sits as quietly as possible in her seat and keeps her head down. Someone else would either say: Sure, I've read it, that *Puntila* play, and I know who Bertolt Brecht is. Then the teacher would ask some more specific questions, and probably the one who had spoken would turn out to have been lying, it would become apparent that he knew nothing at all, neither about *Puntila* nor Bertolt Brecht, and only said so to make the teacher think he was an industrious student, which in any case would mean he was resourceful—or else he would say: No, it's true, I don't know

Puntila, and I don't know who Bertolt Brecht is, either. This would be sheer insolence, and it would mean that the one who had spoken was not timid, in other words that he was lazy but at least courageous, and this, too, would stand him in good stead, at least among his peers. Of course it isn't possible for all the children to be either resourceful or courageous, and there are several who also sit there quietly and keep their heads down, but they cannot possibly sit there just as quietly and keep their heads quite as far down as the girl, because these others, when they are quiet and keep their heads down, do so in the hope of making the teacher overlook their existence so that she will not call on them. The girl, on the other hand, when she sits there so very quietly with her head down is in fact trying to achieve precisely this: being called on by the teacher, being asked why she is sitting there so quietly, whether it is really true that she knows nothing, absolutely nothing at all about *Puntila* or Bertolt Brecht. She is all but forcing the teacher to call on her, her submissive posture produces a sort of suction that attracts the ill will of others, including the teacher. The teacher will have no choice but to ask the girl about *Puntila* and Brecht, although it is plain to see that there is not a single person anywhere in the world likely to know less about *Puntila* and Bertolt Brecht than this lumpy girl seated at this desk. Precisely for this reason she will ask her, so as to embarrass her. She will compel the girl to admit her guilt, choking with shame: It is true, I don't know anything, neither about *Puntila* nor about Bertolt Brecht. And in this way the girl will cause the teacher in her turn to feel ashamed, for having allowed herself to get carried away to the point of harassing the girl thus. The teacher, of course, has no idea that the girl herself has used suction to all but compel her to act as she has. And therefore, while any other student would be punished for this lack of knowledge, the girl will not be punished. The teacher, attempting to justify this leniency to herself, will tell herself that the girl is so fundamentally incapable of knowing anything at all that no punishment can alter her incapacity, that the girl is an absolutely lost cause and that the most fitting thing can only be to give up on her.

I am the weakest. None of these foundlings is weaker than I am.

The girl is terribly clumsy. She cannot even walk properly. While she is attempting to cross the schoolyard, she knocks into children who are playing ball or chatting in little groups—one of the smallest boys grins at her and asks: Are you the new teacher?, belches in her face and scoots off. The girl flees into a side entrance of the school building and has leapt up three wooden steps when she stops short, as if she'd come to a wall: There on the landing a couple is kissing, a tangle of hair and hands and trousers. Suddenly she is unable to see, she looks but sees nothing, it is not only the couple she cannot see, she sees nothing at all, not the stairwell, not the wooden steps, nothing in front of her and nothing behind, nothing. She opens her eyes as wide as she can, but she sees nothing.

The girl doesn't know what word to put in the blank. In her English book there are blanks marked with ellipses, and these blanks are to be filled in with a verb in the correct tense, but the girl doesn't know the correct tense. So she raises her hand. It is the teacher's duty to come over to the girl's desk, bend down and explain the method to her. The girl says Yes and nods, says Oh, I see, and with her eyes follows the teacher's thick, hairy index finger as it moves across the paper. And the moment the teacher has stood up again and turned his back on the girl with an encouraging nod, she will raise her hand again, and she can count on the teacher's once again coming to stand beside her desk, bending down and giving his explanation as he moves his index finger across the paper—he is paid for his patience. To be sure, there are instances when a pupil's stupidity might appear to be a ruse, instilling in the teacher a certain nervousness, a secret irritation which will cost him some effort to keep in check, or if it is not irritation, then it is perhaps doubt that may assail the teacher—doubt as to whether he has chosen the right profession—upon his finding a pupil's head to be as heavy as lead, incapable of absorbing the principles of rational thought. Yet it is neither nervousness, nor irritation, nor self-doubt that assails the teacher when he sees the girl holding up her hand. No, fear and pity make this English teacher tremble as he awaits the girl's signal, and each time her fleshy arm rises above her head, he will betake himself wearily to her side and with the utmost patience, often even with tears in his eyes, will repeat explanations he has already given hundreds of times over one more hopeless time, moving his hairy index finger across the blanks with their ellipses, speaking slowly, ever so slowly, in English, a language the girl will never, ever understand, even when it is spoken ever so slowly. In the teachers' lounge, his impression was confirmed by his colleagues: The girl's incapacity really did extend to all her subjects to the same degree, it was as credible as it was irremediable. She was cutting off her nose to spite her face, the German teacher remarked. The chronically paltry state of the girl's knowledge fills the English teacher with shame, even the sort of guilt that might be felt by a person who enjoys advantages that were attained by some subterfuge and are thus inaccessible to others. He sees himself as a sort of victor *malgré soi* in what is for the girl a hopeless contest. Thus he fails to understand the power of this raised female arm to compel, fails to understand that not only does he respond to her call, he has to respond to it, he is being torn apart—in other words, governed—by the perfectly legitimate expectation that he provide help where it is needed, coupled with his inability to provide it. Thus afflicted with blindness, he will seek to cover up his supposed guilt by addressing the German teacher forcefully on some other occasion: That girl there, he will say, a dead loss.

And so while these and other teachers quickly fall prey to the girl's well-calculated stupidity, because they are looking down at this eighth-grade classroom at such a remove of years they might as well be surveying it from on high, the situation at ground level, that is, seen from the equally valid vantage point of her fellow students, presents itself quite differently. Not that these peers of hers would be any less likely to use an answer cribbed from the lips of others to neutralize a teacher—but outside the classroom, matters appear in a different light. Just as a herd becomes restless when the One of the Cleft Foot enters its midst, these fourteen-year-olds can scent deception the moment it is directed toward them. And while the girl has no trouble making the grown-ups see of her only what she wishes them to see, no more and no less, among those her own age she displays true insecurity, and this provokes them. The girl's massive body only increases the insecurity that makes her tremble, this body practically towers above the horizon, it appears shakier than the other fourteen-year-old bodies, this shakiness is apparent to the others and is felt by them as a provocation.

Around me, everything is awhirl. No one looks at me, I don't know what I have done. These beautiful children with their childish skin, their childish teeth, their thin little bracelets—they slam the gate shut in my face. Why does no one speak to me?

The hoarse voices of adolescent boys crowd in on the girl, whose plumpness was acquired in a place she refuses to name, they ask her: Where were you? Where were you before? And the girl begins to stab at them with a pair of scissors. She stabs only air with her scissors, as the boys are quicker than she is. At the front of the room, a lesson is in progress, while in back the battle rages. Two boys grab the girl by her arms. Desperately she struggles. A third boy tries to put his hand up her skirt. The girl flails about. Shrilly the recess bell sounds.

The girl tears herself loose, the boys charge off, the room empties. The girl remains alone, the scissors still in her hand, and smoothes her skirt down. She packs up her school things and leaves.

The girl is in search of something, she is trying to speak, but while the vocabulary itself appears to have nothing wrong with it, there is always a black, gaping nothingness that can be glimpsed through it, as through filigree. Everything that comes out of her mouth always looks like a lie, even if it isn't one, the girl is always giving her peers the impression that even she cannot believe herself, not even when she is speaking a truth, and then this truth ceases to be true. And when the matter at hand is too trifling for it to be a question of trust or distrust, then the ones to whom the girl has addressed herself will be overcome with boredom, and this boredom, too, originates primarily in the circumstance that even the girl appears bored by what she is saying, more bored than anyone else, as if everything filtered through her person is either sullied or exhausted in the process. It then reappears as a sullied or exhausted entity, and gives quite a different impression than before. As in a chemical reaction, the girl adds to every thought that passes through her head something like an invisible substance which changes the sign preceding it from positive to negative. The sentence that is the thought remains just as it was, and yet the moment the girl utters this sentence, a thought that was perfectly sincere becomes mendacious, and an interesting one descends into tedium. And so most of what the girl says founders almost at once, it drags itself by the hair into the bog no sooner than it appears, no one is obliged to find it credible, not even the girl herself, and this is most painful of all. The girl's sentences lie in her stomach like a heap of scrap metal, they cannot take root inside her, and sometimes she even looks down to see whether one of these sentences isn't poking out of her side.

The geography teacher is slimy, the others declare. In the girl's head, at the spot which in the others is occupied by an opinion of this sort, there is only emptiness. Nonetheless she will undertake the experiment with all the good will in the world, and the moment she catches sight of the geography teacher while she is shuffling down the hallway with all the others, although she realizes that in the spot which in others is occupied by an opinion she has only emptiness, she will venture a comment: Everywhere he goes, she will say, that geography teacher leaves a trail of slime behind him. All the girl wants to do is say what any of the other pupils would have said at just this moment, she wants to contribute to the cohesiveness of this group which she is a part of, but then of course even this modest undertaking proves too much for her. Her sweet little voice fails her the moment she begins to speak, it balks, leaves her in the lurch, presenting itself as a cracking falsetto. Not even a voice can manage to put down roots in this body, which, misleadingly, makes a solid impression. The others, repelled by the inferior manner in which the girl is parroting this view of theirs, will understandably start looking for a new one to replace it with.

The school dreams are returning. Dreams of changing rooms, flooded mass toilets, swimming pools with someone's hair floating into my mouth. Doors being thrust open, slammed shut, suddenly I realize that someone is watching me, someone is peering over one of the flimsy walls that go only halfway up while my piss hits the ground beside the toilet. The colors: mint green and white.

Then the girl, maintaining an appropriate distance from her classmates but mimicking their postures, squats with her back to the wall on the floor outside a classroom, awaiting the arrival of the chemistry teacher. At the moment, her inferiority is the only existing link between her and the others: that she is inadequate and is made to feel this inadequacy quite clearly, but without being able to understand in what this inadequacy consists, that she is guilty and acknowledges this guilt, but without recognizing in what it consists, that she arrives too late and apologizes, but never learns what she has arrived too late for, all these things comprise her relationship to them. When she arrives somewhere, the others are just leaving, and wherever she is, the past is about to begin, the others leave her behind for their own amusement, but she keeps tagging along behind them, like an echo.

The chemistry teacher arrives and unlocks the door to the laboratory. The mob streams in, the girl taking her place next to the boy with the rough-hewn face. The chemistry teacher stations himself behind his lab bench and begins agitating test tubes, combining their contents, holding them up in the air, and describing all that is taking place. He dissolves sodium carbonate in water and, by adding a few drops of phenolph-thalein, causes this formerly clear fluid to turn purple before the astonished eyes of the fourteen-year-olds. Now he will ask: Where did the purple come from?, but no one will know the answer, there will be various whisperings and giggles, and one pupil will attempt to frighten the chemistry teacher by licking the top of his possibly contaminated desk. The girl's face throughout this class session displays contentment, for all that is being asked of her is to watch someone dissolving sodium carbonate in water and adding a few drops of phenolph-thalein to produce a purple coloration, and then someone licking his possibly contaminated desktop, there are no conse-quences to any of this, and soon class is over and everyone leaves, everyone and the girl.

The others are walking, and as they walk they speak among themselves; the girl listens. One girl says to another: Are you going to lunch after? And the other responds to the first: If I have to look at that slop one more time… I could puke just thinking about it. The girl slows her steps, allows herself to fall behind, and further back addresses a classmate, saying to her casually: I'm not going to lunch after, I can't stand to look at that slop, it's enough to make you puke. But the girl she has addressed doesn't say: Me too, or: Oh, I don't think the food is all that bad, or: I have to go to lunch even though it's disgusting, I'm really starving. She doesn't say any of these things, but just stares at the girl, gives a quick grimace and walks away. The girl's face is hot, as if she were suddenly terrified, she glances down at herself and, sure enough, there is the sentence she has stolen from her classmate poking out of her side.

The girl finds her way to the kitchen. She has discovered that if she loiters long enough there on her big feet, she will some-times be given leftovers to eat when all the shifts of classes have finished their meals and some food still remains. Sometimes she has to work for this treat: She might, say, be asked to roll the empty barrels outside for pickup, and although this imme-diately makes her break out in a sweat, she is glad to do it, she likes the crunching sound the barrels make outside on the sand. Then she is allowed to return to the kitchen and stands in a corner to spoon up her reward. As she eats, she gazes at a stained notice that has been affixed to the tiles, this notice contains the Health Department guidelines.

No pain, no gain, the gym teacher admonishes the class at the end of every session, right when they finish their endurance training. This admonition is familiar to the girl, only she can't think from where, clearly it is something someone once imparted to her as a golden rule for life. The girl loves gym class, she thinks it's pretty when all the pupils are dressed uniformly in red and white, teams are chosen, and these teams exist for the purpose of developing team spirit. The girl possesses a great deal of team spirit, but unfortunately her body does not reflect it. On the balance beam, she lumbers about like a pale lump of dough with a head. The teacher has to force herself to look up at her. She cannot help but marvel at this creature. The creature is performing a languorous dance upon the balance beam. The primordial transition from water to land. Or else the girl runs and runs and runs, and at the end of this long race she is as pale as a sheet of paper. She isn't sure whether she will have to collapse right away, or whether she can put off this collapse until the teacher has said: Next!, she does her best to remain standing so as not to disgrace her team, but in the end when she cannot hold out any longer and measures her length in the wet grass, the teacher says the thing about pain and gain. After several gym classes, the girl realizes to her distress that merely summoning up the good will she brings to her team is already such a drain on her resources that a definite decrease in strength can be noted. This good will appears to stand in a precisely inverse proportion to what can be achieved by it. This good will is hung about one like chains and impedes all forward motion. The girl has the good will, indeed the best will, not to disgrace her team, but nonetheless she becomes slower from week to week. Maybe what she needs is a fortissimo, she tells herself, maybe she's just been running too softly.

On her way back outside, her gym bag trailing along on the ground behind her, the girl stops and stands inside the entryway to the gymnasium where the fire safety code is posted. She studies the fire safety code, and this allows her to forget her exhaustion—after every gym class she studies the fire safety code, and this makes her calm again. Meanwhile her class-mates are filing outside behind her back, many of them are slurping milk out of milk cartons, because gym class has made them thirsty, they chatter, gossip and laugh, their voices vanish through the glass door, a cold draft breezes through the entryway, and the girl tries to recall the names that go with these voices, but she isn't yet able to do so. She doesn't know her classmates well enough, she cannot yet remember their names.

While she is helping the kitchen staff dry the last of the plates, the girl hears someone doing something out in the dining hall, she sticks her head through the hatch which, only an hour ago, was being used to dish out food, and sees the custodian hanging up a large map of the world, he is hanging it up back to front, with the blank side facing forward. Meanwhile a second man, one the girl doesn't know, is moving the chairs and tables around, and then the two of them together lift a large piece of apparatus onto one of the tables. Finally the custodian climbs up on a ladder and drapes a large black cloth over the windows, the other man helping. While he is climbing down, the custodian notices the girl watching him through the hatch. He says: Careful, don't stick your neck out too far, the window might fall down and chop your head off. He's expecting this to make the girl laugh. His expectations are not met. Pointing to the apparatus, he says: That's for the movie. Today is movie day. Then he goes out into the hall to unlock the glass door. A large number of children come in, they have been waiting outside, all the children are coming, including all the girl's classmates, all of them knew that today was movie day, all of them except the girl, since no one told her. The girl abandons her plate and comes from behind the hatch. She looks to see where there is still room, spies a table off to one side that already has two children sitting on it, and shuffles over to it without lifting her head, in a transport of happiness she hops onto the table, which isn't so easy. Then everything goes dark, and the show begins. First, an old wooden cottage appears on the screen, then one of its shutters is shoved open from the inside, and an old peasant woman leans out of the window and starts telling a fairy tale. Now cottage and peasant woman dissolve, and the story proper begins. It is a very sad story, and the girl begins to cry, she cannot help it, but she weeps softly so as not to disturb the others, tears drip from her chin down onto her plump hands, which she is holding clasped in her lap. She gazes and gazes, and only after quite some time has passed does she realize that the others are laughing at precisely those bits that make her cry, a few of them aren't even looking at the screen at all, but instead are pushing and shoving one another about in the best of spirits. Now the girl stops crying and carefully observes all that is happening there in the dark, then she wipes the tears from her chin as inconspicuously as possible and begins to swing her legs gently to and fro. The wooden cottage has just reappeared on the screen, this time as seen from within, and one can observe a battle in progress. Several men are attempting to drive the peasant woman from her house, but she fights back, shouting again and again: Over my dead body! Over my dead body! Hereupon one of the men draws his gun and shoots her. Now they are carrying the dead woman out of the house on a bier, and the ownership of the cottage passes to the men. The connection between this scene and the fairy tale itself is lost on the girl, but she finds it all terribly funny. She tries to show her teeth when she laughs, like the others, but laughter itself, the sound of laughter, is no longer familiar to her. The little boy sitting next to the girl notices the hoarse raspy sounds she is making, so she falls silent.

Meanwhile the girl's number has been sewn into all her clothes, her number is 9912. The child who arrived at the

Home just before her has the number 9911, and there is some other one, one who arrived after, who has the number 9913, this is a perfectly ordinary series. The girl adapts to the various procedures that determine the course of life in the Home, but above all her inward submission is flawless, she practically obeys commands before they are issued. While all the other adolescents have a greater or lesser degree of talent in following instructions, with the girl it seems not to be a matter of following at all, rather it is as if she herself knows what an asset such discipline is. Should, for instance, the instructress performing the weekly inspection happen to snatch all the clothing out of a locker and throw it on the floor because it was not stacked neatly enough, this will never be clothing belonging to the girl. And when the instructress then pulls the delinquent over to her by the hair, whispering: All of my pupils are dear to me, all of them except you! this will surely not be the girl's hair. In such cases the girl will be found standing before her locker in which all the clothing is neatly stacked, observing these events out of the corner of one eye.

To the other pupils, this infallibility seems a form of betrayal, because there is something slavish about it, and because among slaves nothing is deadlier than for one of their number to voluntarily assume the slave's role. But while the girl's desire for order happens to correspond to the standards imposed by the pedagogical staff, its origins are quite different. The girl sees her stack of clothes, which is comprehensible to her, in relation to all that appears to her incomprehensible and thus hostile. Disorder of every sort is hostile, this begins with those objects that, precisely because they weren't stacked neatly in a cupboard, fall out at you when you open the door, but it ends in putrefaction, death and confusion, things the girl refuses to think about. She is able to withstand this onslaught of hostilities by arranging her stack of clothes in such a way that it remains comprehensible. It is more than her own tidiness she is preserving by these means, but of this no one, as yet, has even an inkling. And if one or the other pupil should be struck dead by the objects falling out at him from his locker, or else by one of the teaching staff after discovering this disorder during locker inspection, this will quite simply no longer be plausible as an expression of the destructive principle once the girl has succeeded in wresting some bit of territory, tiny as it may be, from the control of this destructive principle, hereby establishing the simultaneous existence of disorder and order. This simultaneousness robs the calamity—one whose very essence is that there's no escaping it, no escaping it as a matter of principle—of its ability to exist.

But precisely this: the fact that the girl has never once come to the attention of the teaching staff during locker inspection, has attracted the attention of her peers. Her roommates, investigating this matter, examined the inside of her locker. The first thing they discovered was that even in the middle of the week, when no inspections take place, the clothes in the girl's locker lie neatly stacked, as though she never touched her locker or used any of the things contained in it, though of course she did have to get dressed every day and take out and replace certain school items. Secondly, the locker contains nothing more and nothing less than it did on her first day at the Home, nothing has been added which might allow the others to infer some human sentiment in the girl. The locker's metal doors are as bare as ever, not a sticker, not a photo, not a poster adorns them, though the Home's administration allows the decoration of locker doors—nothing, nothing, nothing. To the three others, it seemed practically inhuman that the girl's life should have left no traces where it was being spent. There must be a hiding place, they thought, and started rummaging through everything, but there was no hiding place.

During recess the next day, a few of the girl's classmates grab hold of her and the boy with greasy hair who had to repeat a grade, the class reject, and lead the two of them off to a distant corner of the schoolyard, beneath the chestnut trees, out of the range of vision of the teacher on duty. There they place a bicycle lock, stiff as the jaws of a trap, around both of their necks and lock them together. They had to make the girl bend over a little, for she is too tall even for this sort of jest. Then they run off. The girl and the boy with greasy hair have to stand there listening as the dry leaves of the chestnut trees tumble to the ground.

The weight of my life is increasing. Above me I erect a splendid palace. My palace is made of straw. It stands upon a hen's foot, I slaughtered the hen myself. When it storms, you can still hear its shrieks. I ornament my palace. It will make a beautiful bonfire.

The girl knows that her body is a transgression, she would like to atone for it, and so she obeys the decrees issued by her classmates to the letter. Thus she willingly stands with her eyes closed in the middle of the sports field, waiting for the others to hide and then call to her. But then they do not call, and not just for a quarter of an hour, but for many hours on end, at first because they have permitted themselves a joke at her expense, and later out of sheer forgetfulness, but the girl remains standing there all these many hours, first while the joke is being had at her expense, and later when she has simply been forgotten, for she stubbornly refuses to violate a decree, even after she herself has had to realize that it is only a joke being played on her, indeed the very decree itself was a joke, and even when it dawns on her with a probability bordering on certainty that sheer forgetfulness is to blame for this decree's not having been revoked. And when she observes that she will catch cold if she remains standing there for even a little while longer, she nevertheless refuses to violate the decree.

And so she remained standing in the place assigned to her and did not stir from it and thus she caught a cold. And at dusk a staff member found her still standing there and shouted at her whether she had lost her wits to be standing there like that and led her away. Don't you want to be able to have children some day? the teacher shouted, and with all his shouting failed to hear that the girl had quietly responded: No.

After this, the girl is sent to the infirmary to drink herb tea for a few days, take steam baths, and warm up again. The girl is happy. The infirmary asks nothing but repose for and of its patients, and for the sake of this repose, beds have been provided, freshly made beds with oversized pillows in which you can bury yourself. The girl doesn't have to move, indeed she is not allowed to, movement of any kind is forbidden. She is allowed to sleep, indeed required to sleep, as much as she can, and sleeping is one of the few areas in which the girl has achieved a high level of proficiency. All the rules that previously applied have now been suspended for as long as she lies here in her infirmary bed and is allowed, indeed required to sleep. There is no place from which the world appears farther removed than from an infirmary room such as this one. It is a place where one is sheltered, and what one is being sheltered from is, of course, the world, what else. One lies beneath the eiderdown and everything loud, everything pointy or bright, everything that might possibly beset one is repelled by this soft bulwark. To be sure, there are intrusions, in the form of measuring instruments, for example the thermometer, which is cold, but it would never cross the girl's mind to refuse them entry. When her temperature is taken, for example, she learns that it is precisely 39.2 degrees Celsius, and so her body loses a little of its monstrous incomprehensibility. This, too, makes it agreeable to be confined to the infirmary, for here there is a staff that is familiar with the mechanics of the human body. This body that might appear to its owner like a mound of flesh living its own life in a disorderly, even malevolent way, with no sense of why in the first place, or from where, or for how much longer, this body whose whims one is at the mercy of, which hurts, catches cold or gets infections, which begins to smell bad if not regularly washed and whose weight, even when it happens not to have a cold or an infection, nor to smell bad, is a burden one must bear without understanding it— this very body is here receiving the appropriate treatment as a matter of course. With relief, the girl thus recognizes that she must have more or less the same body as everyone else, leaving aside its lack of beauty, which is merely external. On the inside, then, her body is nothing out of the ordinary, and the illnesses that assail it are nothing out of the ordinary, and here one finds these specialists who know the girl's body just as well as all other bodies and administer to it just the same appropriate treatment as to all the others, because it is always one and the same mechanism. They ask only those questions which they ask always of everyone, and shortly thereafter they issue instructions that are just the same as they would issue in any other case and prescribe just what they would prescribe in any other such case under similar circumstances, and ask nothing not directly pertinent to the illness at hand. What concerns them is this machine, which is always the same: the heart, which is located in the upper left quadrant in every individual, or the lymph nodes, which are always to be found beneath the ears. This is what interests them. But what sort of figure one presents during the examination, whether one is huge, rough or even hideous, whether one is stupid or extremely stupid, all these things do not interest them, particularly not when all the signs are pointing unambiguously to a head cold. This happy staff, these happy specialists, they alone are able to relieve a living creature, at least briefly, of the great responsibility of having always to sustain this life that has been given one, always with only oneself to rely on, and without even knowing to what end. They say: Take a steam bath once a day, or: Take two of these tablets three times a day, or: Stay in bed, or: Drink only this herb tea and do not eat anything for the time being. And you don't have to lose any thought over the matter, let alone come up with the idea yourself that it would be best to take a steam bath once a day, or two of these tablets thrice daily, or stay in bed or drink herb tea and not eat anything for the time being. All you have to do is lie there, following the instructions of these people for whom life is a machine, and sleep a great deal. You can give yourself up to them entirely and, for once, turn your back on life.

The staff open the door to the girl's infirmary room without knocking, they pull back the sheets, various procedures are carried out, the girl's body is probed without anyone asking permission, measurements are taken and developments moni-tored, and the girl doesn't have to feel ashamed, for once she is permitted a furlough from shame, because it would make no sense at all to feel ashamed for having the same mechanism inside her as everyone else, she can be certain that no one here takes the least interest in whether or not she feels shame, what with her dark body itself lying spread out, open for inspection before the eyes of the specialists.

And so the girl rests in peace, she dozes or else sleeps, moving as little as possible, and warms herself beneath the heavy bedclothes. She is beginning to smell nice. The smell of her shapeless body vanishes almost completely, and in its place the aromas of health arrive, the smell of herb tea, the smell of the starched bedclothes and above all the smell of the disinfectants whose frequent use is the ambition of every hospital worker. The girl wallows in well-being as she thinks of the tiny para-sites that inhabit her as they do every other person, parasites who now are in for it: these incarnations of the most vulgar gluttony. Teeming, invisible filth that is now being driven off, driven off by corrosive, caustic, radical measures. The girl gulps down the tablets that have been prescribed to help her fight off her cold, and then there is nothing left for her to do but lie there in the knowledge that these inhabitants of her interior are now in for it. From time to time nurses appear who lead the girl out from beneath her eiderdown, but when they take her by the hand, it is only to bring her to have her steam bath, and this does the girl good, she sweats everything that is sick within her out of her body, everything that is dirty, indeed one might almost say she is sweating her body out of her body. And when she returns from the steam bath to her bed, she can see how the bedclothes have twisted into a corkscrew to release her, the bedclothes lie in a sort of whirlpool, a sort of maelstrom, yet nothing at all has happened.

Beneath the covers it is very warm, warmer than anywhere else. Outside the bedclothes, in the infirmary room, even in the hallway of the infirmary, it is still warmer than usual, that is, warmer than is usual for a public or private building. It is somewhat less warm in the other areas of the Home, the dormitories, washrooms, activity rooms and sports facilities and the corridors that link them, yet here, too, it is still fairly warm, warm enough for one to exist under humane conditions. Throughout the grounds of the Home, the temperature can be described even in winter as perfectly reasonable, while outside the fenced-in grounds, beneath this self-same sky but outside the fence, this is not the case, that is one of the few facts from the past the girl can still recall quite clearly. And a reasonable temperature is one of those things that contribute to one's survival. The girl is quick to feel a chill, even in summer she feels chilly more often than the others, although she carries around much more fat on her than they do, such that one might be inclined to assume her fat would keep her warm. And when the others are unwilling to believe her when she says she's freezing, she shows them her arms, on which the little hairs are standing straight up with the cold, and when they continue to gaze skeptically into her blushing face, the girl plays her trump, which is her ability to make her teeth chatter at any time, and this is the decisive proof.

So she's freezing, and she has to sneeze, unusually often she is subject to sneezing fits that arrive suddenly and without warning. Even when she isn't sneezing, a droplet can frequently be found hanging from her nose, indicating that she suffers from a chronic sniffle. Even in summer, in the middle of summer, when everyone else has forgotten there is such a thing as the sniffles, the girl has to curl into a ball at her desk to blow her nose. She curls up to blow her nose which had a droplet hanging from it, because she is ashamed, not only of having the sniffles, but also of the old, disintegrating scrap of tissue she is using as a handkerchief. Even her sniffles are sniffles on the lowermost rung of the hierarchy, unworthy sniffles that make the mucus flow out of her nose like an old lady's, not an ordinary cold such as makes people's noses stuffy for a week, forcing them to breathe through their mouths, and then it's over, no, nor is her sneezing ever a lovely, liberating explosion, rather it is practically feline, a stifled, spasmodic snuffling, as if it were a cat sneezing.

Even apart from this sniffling, the girl's health is quite fragile, in marked contrast to what her stature might lead one to expect. To be sure, you can tell at once that this girl is not an athlete, and that she therefore is not likely to number among those who are particularly hardy, but to how great an extent she is in fact susceptible to every sort of mundane and, as will later become clear, more serious illness is not immediately apparent when you first see her, the impression she makes is far too robust. Her form, which gives an initial impression of repleteness, leads one to infer solidity within. But as it turns out, just the opposite is true: The reason her body has swollen out of all proportion is that it is unable to utilize appropriately the substances provided it in great quantity thanks to the girl's voracious appetite. On closer inspection, it appears this body is simply accumulating without rhyme or reason all that has ever been introduced into it, as though misguided stinginess made it unwilling to surrender anything at all, as though the

49

body itself were merely a great, blind cache, a stock-pile whose contents, however, cannot be put to use because the instructions are missing—the impression one has is of a ruinous mass, one that is alive, to be sure, for a body must necessarily be alive, but at the same time somehow dead.

And perhaps it simply isn't true that it is out of immoderate-ness that the girl must eat so much, as the others always claim with disgust, perhaps it is her only chance at survival. It isn't true that all this food allows her to survive much better than the others—she is barely surviving—it's just that she has to eat far more in comparison with the others in order to preserve at least some degree of life despite this difficult body of hers, which is lacking even the most fundamental powers of resist-ance. For example, the girl has only to spend a quarter of an hour sitting in a draft, perhaps because the teacher is airing out the classroom, which, no one knows why, smells of rubber, and already she can count on her neck becoming stiff for the entire next week, her sniffle worsening, and her ears beginning to ache. And naturally this earache is no run-of-the-mill earache, of course not, it will invariably be accompanied by a whistling sound that only the girl can hear, inside her. The music teacher made her sing this sound for him, and he iden-tified it as F-sharp two octaves above middle C.

Leaving aside the pain, which an illness brings to the girl just as it would to anyone else, time spent being sick is generally considered disagreeable because it is nothing but a waiting period, empty time. Children get bored to death and spit out the herb tea because they find its taste insipid, and when they are older, they will describe the experience as having been chained to their beds. Bed, however, and the notion of being practically chained to it, are things to which the girl has no objections whatever, bed is without a doubt the safest place in the world, and what is more, one of the warmest. Nonetheless, there is something unattractive about being sick, something embarrassing, and this is the interruption of quotidian existence which the illness brings about, the special status that someone who is frequently ill must necessarily acquire. Of this, the girl is ashamed. You might almost say that it is her shame over being sick so often, more often than the others, this fear of not appearing normal, this embarrassment that is the real torment, and you might almost assume it to be this embarrassment that makes the girl ill so often, a diabolical cycle. And all the while she is feeling the most intense longing for an infirmary bed. It would be conceivable that her frequent absences from school might lend her a certain standing among her fellow pupils, that she might begin to appear somehow anarchistic if the others assumed she was only playing truant in a particularly cunning way. This might cost her the lowermost rung in the hierarchy which has so miraculously come into her possession and which is, moreover, the safest one, possibly she would rise to a higher rank and then have to prove herself worthy of it, from then on she would be tested for her suitability, since every rank, every rank except the lowermost one, is defined by ability, not inability. The girl would be wrenched from the warm comfort of having been forgotten and would be forced to act. It might also be that through this excess of illness she might accidentally begin to arouse pity after all, that the others might begin to go easy on her, to stop pushing her down, and from this moment on the girl would be condemned to life as a foreign body, all her efforts to achieve normalcy through failure would be vanquished once the pity began. All these thoughts taken together cause such horror to erupt within the girl that it makes her ill, ill once more—her customary sniffles are joined by a fever which leads her by the most direct possible path to a bed in the infirmary. And there, ensconced once more in her infirmary bed, she is overcome by a feeling of the most immense, undisguised joy.

In this respect, then, the girl is defined by contradictions which she attempts to escape all the more urgently as soon as she is no longer ill. For example, she likes very much to join, dressed like all the others, washed like all the others, the group of pupils who pour out of the school building once classes have ended to go to the dining hall. And she succeeds in this, though all the others are walking in pairs or small groups, chattering among themselves, and she herself is walking alone since no one has any interest in talking to her, nonetheless she succeeds in leaving the building as a part of this group, nonetheless she contributes her share to the throng and its odor, the throng and the odor of eighth-grade pupils on their way to the dining hall after school. This pale, huge creature sits down with the others at the food-stained table, at the eighth-grade table, among all her classmates, no one can object to that, and if someone does object to it, it will be at most a sort of mockery that is internal to the table, the eighth-grade table, a clarification of the table's internal coalitions, a negative sort of recognition, but recognition nonetheless, perhaps she will even be received as a glutton with welcoming jeers. It may happen that someone spits in her food, but she doesn't have to sit alone, doesn't have to be a loner, doesn't have to be anything out of the ordinary. The others watch as she silently shovels the food into her mouth, on some days she even goes so far as to ask whether she may finish off the scraps remaining on their plates should something be left over, gnaw the bones, lick up the sauces, clean out the pudding bowls with her finger, suck the last flat drops from their drink cartons. Tormented by the most intense cravings, she is able, on lucky days, to come by these eighth-grade leftovers, she eats that of which the others have eaten, drinks that of which the others have drunk, this purifies her blood. Whereas generally she is colorless, nearly to the point of invisibility, the concentration she brings to the activity of eating gives her the appearance of having character. Thus while the girl arouses the displeasure and disgust of those before whose eyes she is eating so immoderately, she is nonetheless partaking in the general conviviality, and this displeasure and this disgust are quite ordinary displeasure and disgust, they are perfectly quotidian, the cruelty her classmates are particularly fond of doling out during mealtimes is a perfectly normal cruelty, one the girl can count on, it is cruelty to which she is entitled, and above all it is not nothing. Occasionally someone will bring up the bucket of pigs' eyes that had appeared beside the teacher's desk the morning a dissection was on the program in biology class. The eyes had been distributed among the class so that each pupil really did have an eye of his own, and it was astonishing what exertion was needed to penetrate the tough outer membrane with a scalpel—when this had been achieved, the fluid from inside the pig's eye ran over their hands. The girl eats silently and with great appetite without once looking up from her plate, her thorough chewing motions punctuated by hiccups, stubborn uninhibited hiccups, such as only children get. At such moments it is quite possible that someone seated directly across from the girl will feel the urgent need to rip the Band-Aid from the oozing fever blister on his upper lip and display to the girl this festering wound, asking whether she knows of a good cure for his malady. The girl is imperturbable, virtually bovine, she says she doesn't know of any cure and while speaking continues to chew her sausage, her vegetables, she gives the upper lip a cursory glance, but does not meet the gaze of the one who has asked her advice, the hiccups are still not under control, she chews, and she has placed both elbows protectively around her plate on which she has piled a quite respectable portion. Like an ox that has been hitched before a plow, she plods onward, says no, she doesn't know of any cure, and this answer is utterly unsullied, absolutely pure, for while it has already been demonstrated on many occasions that the others can be expected to treat her unkindly, that the others are incapable of being well-disposed toward her, she nonetheless shows herself again and again to be astonishingly proficient at forgetting this. Just as a puddle into which a stone has been thrown is able shortly afterward to entrust itself to gravity once more and form a level surface, the girl, too, possesses just such an earth-bound, unsulliable nature. Thus the jokes made at her expense must be particularly crude if they are to have an effect at all and not just pass by unnoticed. To the amazement and general amusement of all, on the other hand, it was discovered that pranks whose effectiveness has already been proven can be repeated over and over again absolutely unchanged without the girl's learning over time to parry them with greater skill. For example, the others once succeeded in taking away her plate of food during a meal by asking her to clap her hands. She didn't attempt to defend herself, just sat there and quietly began to cry. Never would it have occurred to her to leap from her seat and try to get her plate back, never would she have begun to fight, although her chances would surely have been quite good considering her size. Eventually she stopped crying. When the next day someone asked her to clap her hands while she was eating, she of course did so, and of course her plate was taken away from her once more, and so on. It is hardly conceivable that anyone could be so forgetful. While the others spend their lives amassing hidden thoughts and deriving logical consequences from the comparison of different events, the girl is honing her skills in the art of forgetting.

The less the girl speaks, the less she can do wrong. And, as eventually becomes clear, there are various ways in which she can succeed by her silence. Once during gym class the underpants that had just been allocated to her were stolen, the single pair of underpants that is hers for the week, and the weather is beginning to turn cold, the first snow has fallen. So all she had to put on was her skirt and her stockings, and now the wind can slip beneath her skirt unhindered, already it seems she is beginning to catch cold. The next day, the girl sees five boys from her class playing soccer with her underpants during recess. After this, there is no sign of them, but when another three days have passed she finds a note in her schoolbag with a drawing of her underpants and the words: You've swept all day, now put it away! It takes the girl three hours to decipher this message, then she calmly walks over to the dormitory building, climbs the two flights of stairs to the floor where her room is, and walks down the linoleum of the windowless corridor all the way to the end, to where the broom closet is. She opens the door to the broom closet, the smell of floor wax rises to greet her, and, lo: there are her underpants, stretched atop a broom standing upside down in the corner. The girl plucks her underpants from the broom and, right there in the closet, pulls them up under her skirt.

Jenny Erpenbeck

A few days later chance will have it that the girl surprises the five underpant thieves, appearing as if out of thin air upon the wooded hill behind the Home from which she can see every-thing, just as they have begun to work over a small boy from the third grade. Four of the five are holding him down, and the fifth is kneeling above him and appears to be stuffing his mouth with dirt. Even before the five can release the smaller boy, the girl has already turned around and vanished. All week long the five boys are terrified of the girl, they avoid looking at her so as to keep their fear in check. Boys who attack a third-grader five against one fall without question into the category of juvenile delinquent, and delinquents are sent to an institution designed especially for their ilk, where life is far less pleasant than in the Home, that's what the five are afraid of. But nothing happens, the girl does not report what she has seen, despite the fact that she is clearly, for the moment, in a position of strength. She must be blind or else simply too stupid to commit even an act of revenge requiring so little effort, at least that's what the boys conclude in light of the mercy that has been shown them by their victim. From the girl's perspective, however, these two incidents—the theft of the underpants, and the free-for-all in the woods—do not appear to be related to one another. It is as if she is altogether lacking in self-interest. Each of the events exists for her in its

58

own right, as if a bridge in her head—the one that in most cognizant beings links what has been done to them to what they do to others—has collapsed.

In any case the girl has a great deal of trouble deriving independent thoughts from something she has seen, this has often enough become apparent during various class sessions. And where it is a matter of thought becoming speech, that is, thought's pointing to something beyond itself, even being translated into action, such as is necessary for a betrayal, then there is little to be feared from her. In this particular case there is the additional complication that in order to carry out this betrayal the girl would have to go to the teachers' lounge, the designated location for communicating such complaints— and for her, entering the teachers' lounge is something that lies beyond the realm of possibility, even if she wanted to she wouldn't manage it, for the teachers' lounge lies at the far end of the ground-floor corridor, and this corridor approaches infinity, at least that's how it appears to the girl. The teachers' lounge is beyond her reach, just looking down the corridor makes her dizzy. She stands at her end of the corridor like a fish behind the glass wall of an aquarium—the fish, too, is simply unable to swim through the glass, it, too, has no alter-native but to remain silent, and thus if you know the girl it is in no way surprising that she didn't talk, didn't recognize her advantage when it presented itself or at the very least didn't make use of it. It is thanks to her that the machinations of her classmates remain hidden from sight.

The week after she, who knows why, didn't say anything, kept her mouth shut, as her schoolmates say with already something verging on respect, one of the boys from the fifth-grade corridor comes flying across the courtyard, pursued by a teacher. The girl is just taking a scrap of something from her pocket to blow her nose when the one being pursued stumbles over her in full gallop while glancing back at his pursuer. But instead of cursing and giving the girl an additional kick as might ordinarily happen, he simply gets up without a word, and in a desperately foolhardy impulse presses money into the girl's moist hand, the stolen money, apparently, because of which he is being pursued. Hastily he whispers something to the girl and then dashes off. The girl is holding the money in one hand, her ragged handkerchief in the other, and her nose is running. She follows the boy with her eyes for a moment, then looks in the other direction to where the teacher, having just abandoned his pursuit of the boy for want of strength, gazes after the miscreant in exhaustion. The teacher does not see the girl, even though she is in his line of sight, he looks right through her to where the fugitive is standing, and even if he saw her, it would never occur to him that this creature might have anything whatever to do with the troublemaker's plot. Now the girl doesn't know whose money she is holding in her hand, whether it is the teacher's or that of a fellow student. What the boy on the run whispered to her was: Hold on to this! And so the girl, without a thought, puts the money in her pants pocket, she neither wonders anything nor does she speak, she simply puts this money, which doesn't interest her, in her pocket, then finally blows her nose using both hands and afterward stuffs the handkerchief on top of the money. And at just this moment she remembers something, remembers something for the first time. She remembers that the name of the boy who has just whispered to her is Björn.

This very day at dusk, the money thief named Björn takes a stroll over to the playground where the girl spends evening after evening perched in solitude upon a metal bar, motionless as a hen that has already tucked its beak beneath its wing for the night. But when Björn walks up to her and holds out his hand, the hen begins to stir, without getting down from the bar she reaches into her pocket and retrieves, in turn, first the handkerchief and then the money, the latter she hands over to her classmate while returning the handkerchief to its place. He counts the money, none of it is missing.

Thus it has been demonstrated: the girl can be put to use. From this moment on, the girl senses a shifting of the fronts, a sort of collective change in the direction of the wind, the cause of which remains obscure to her. The sensation is agreeable. Instinctively she tries to do everything just the way she did on this day when, for the first time ever, a classmate whispered something to her. Blind and happy, she stands here with this warm breeze wafting over her and doesn't want to move ever again. She refuses to surrender the sweater she wore this week to the laundry collection, she won't let them cut her hair—the important thing is that along with the various other habits she unnecessarily retains, she also continues her habit of not speaking. She settles into silence without realizing that her silence is the first thing about her that her classmates have ever prized.

When the girl first entered the Home, it felt to her as if she were attempting to dive into a body of water. She never perceived a single face in isolation, but rather only a flood of faces, and she rowed. Now that she has apparently succeeded in diving beneath the surface in a modest, quiet way, now that she is being allowed to swim with the current, she begins to encounter various distinct individuals. From this moment on, this moment when she is able to hold in her memory the knowledge that one of her classmates is named Björn, she begins to retain other stories as well. Her head ceases to be empty, it is now a head containing the stories of a fourteen-year-old girl.

The first thing she notices are the ink-stained hands of the boy who sits next to her, the one with the rough-hewn face. And once she has compared these hands, not without a certain shame, to her own hands, which are pale and free of stains, her eyes wander up to the rough-hewn face. The boy, no doubt hoping to contain a nosebleed, has stuffed a plug of paper into his right nostril. Then the girl unexpectedly remembers that once, in physics class, this boy constructed an astonishing electrical contraption, a contraption that, when you pushed a button, made countless little lamps light up. As if she has only now attained the peace of mind to cobble together these fragments, the girl finds herself unexpectedly able to understand various things that had heretofore bewildered her. She observes her neighbor with the plug in his nose, twisting her head up to peer at him without, however, ceasing to keep it hunched between her shoulders, and recognizes him as a being possessed of unusual powers of invention and technical insight. The ink-stained hands and the plug are just as much a part of this person as is the astonishing electrical contraption, at any rate they suggest that for this particular person other things are more important than a well-groomed appearance. This person is named Erik. Suddenly she knows the name of her neighbor beside whom she has sat for three entire months without once daring to look at him, let alone remember him, and she will no longer forget the namesof the others, either. The girls with whom she shares a room are named Mandy, Nicole and Babette. Many in the Home have names like this, suggesting that names were the only things that could be had for no money when they came into this world. Mandy is tiny, like a dwarf, Nicole has blond hair, and Babette has a cross hanging around her neck and secretly says the Lord's Prayer before she goes to bed.

It has grown cold, the asphalt roads of the Home are covered with watery snow, the sky is full of sulfur, and an icy wind is tearing the last rotten leaves from the poplars along the avenue, crossing the grounds in a straight line without curves of any sort, as if to illustrate the idea of discipline. For the girl, this is the beginning of the Golden Age.

The girl learns to play skat. The young people sit in the class-room, the teacher speaks, and the young people play skat. This skat game takes place between several rows of desks, with the pupils seated in the rows closest to the front half-turning their heads toward the back of the room, they glance over their shoulders at the discard pile and nonchalantly add cards of their own. The game is pursued heartlessly, boldly, indiffer-ently, depending on which teacher is fighting his lonesome battle at the front of the room with the help of a greater or lesser degree of violence. Eighteen!, Twenty!, the pupils hiss under their breaths, while, for example, a slimy, worn-out voice is going on about the quantities of crude oil found in the region around Baku. The teacher can pull his pupils' hair if he thinks he will achieve something in this way, but he will achieve nothing at all.

The young people are blowing notes to one another contain-ing things that could just as well be discussed during recess, in the opinion of the teacher with bleached-blond hair, but in this she is mistaken. Now that the girl's vision is sharper and she is less frightened, she can see these notes flying about, see what invisible lines are being stretched across the classroom, and she begins to speculate as to the contents of these epistles. She waits for the faint explosive sound that accompanies the launch of one of these conspiratorial little balls of paper, and joins the others in giggling over the teacher's impotence to stop these projectiles. For the first time in all her months here, she can be seen giggling with all her heart. Her neighbor Erik is already at work on a catapult for these wadded-up communications, though he is also in possession of a mechanical pencil whose tube might be used to propel this airborne mail. He has already made a sketch of the catapult, and now it is only a matter of completing its construction while the teacher is transferring a complicated diagram onto the blackboard with her back to the students. A few of them are laughing at the teacher's all too short leather skirt, from which two alarmingly bowed legs protrude. The topic of the lesson is subject and predicate. The teacher is marking everything she wishes to have recognized as a subject with a double underline. Her hands are finely powdered with chalkdust, and beneath the chalkdust her skin is splitting.

The contact between the girl and the others becomes closer over the course of the winter, even though it has nothing to do with shared tastes and aversions, or with any commonality of cowardice or courage, rather it can be likened to the intimacy between a man and the factotum who delivers his messages, between a conspirator and the guards posted before his door, between a mistress and her maidservant. The girl begins to do things that might lead one to suspect that her devotion to her classmates borders on idiocy. For example, she makes use of the time allotted to the pupils during a test to copy out the correct answers in a tidy hand for her classmates and surreptitiously pass them to the interested parties. What is surprising is that the girl is suddenly, who knows how, more and more often in possession of the correct answers, and surprising, too, is her ability, only now become apparent, to mimic the handwriting of others well enough to deceive. It remains a mystery, on the other hand, why she displays no interest at all in turning in the correct answers herself.

The girl appears to be content in her mute devotion to her classmates, and when these classmates wage war among themselves, she can reliably be found standing, unencumbered by any opinion of her own, on the side of those who have found a way to use her for their purposes, and when both sides find a way to use her, she is on both sides at once. Since all that is required of her is to hold on to what has been entrusted to her, or say what she has been asked to learn by heart, this is perfectly feasible. The place she occupies in the classroom hostilities is therefore not always an honorable one, it isn't really a place for a human being at all, since it forces one to approach zero, all one's insides must be emptied out like a fish before frying, and only then will there be sufficient space for storing the misdeeds of others, others' happiness and others' grief. But the girl already had such a space within her when she arrived at the Home, she has the heart of a maidservant, and fortune has decreed that she should now find employment among her classmates.

While not long ago the girl herself fell into the cesspool because she was chasing after the others and failed to notice the flimsy board that had been laid across the pit and camouflaged with foliage, she is now one of those who lure new pupils across this board. And then she laughs, opens her mouth up wide to show her teeth and laughs soundlessly but with all her heart.

Now she can be seen trotting across the grounds like a horse, bearing a smaller child on her shoulders, the way one of the older pupils might give a younger sibling a piggyback ride. She is seen running about the dormitory building of the lower school in costume, clutching the top of her head with both hands to keep her crown of feathers—which doesn't quite fit—from falling off, behind her a throng of whooping Indians. She is seen playing hopscotch with the younger children although her feet are so large they barely fit between the lines that have been scraped out in the snow. Her classmates have initiated her into the family structures they have invented for themselves. Each of them has a little brother or sister in one of the lower grades for whom he is responsible. The younger child is subordinate to the older one and must obey him, but in return the older one protects him from the teachers and staff, retaliates for wrongs done to him, takes revenge. But the girl has somehow misunderstood this system, she seems not to have fully understood that its structure is hierarchical, for instead of finding herself a little brother or sister to be her subordinate, she begins to play with the younger pupils, not impatiently or with intent to instruct, the way older pupils generally play with younger ones, but wordlessly and with abandon, as among equals. During recess she goes sliding with the little ones down the slope the first hard frost has coated with ice while her classmates stand in two corners of the schoolyard, furtively smoking. The girls stand in one corner, in the other the boys. From both corners, their incredulous glances follow the girl as she slides down the icy slope with the younger children, but they speak of more important things. After school, too, the girl can be seen sliding once more, like a scarecrow, her arms held wide to help her keep her balance. Until nightfall she remains, and in the end she is completely alone, as the time for the little ones' supper has passed.

There had always been jokes of a certain sort concerning the girl, jokes having to do with her size and bulk which were therefore never quite innocent. For while the girl did not have large breasts, such as would have been fitting for such a body, but rather just two modest little peaks, there was a certain wobble there, a definite flaccidity, and this had sufficed to arouse the fourteen-year-old boys. They themselves were unable to understand what it was that had abruptly caused their revulsion to give way to lust, filling them with the urge to get rough with her. But now that the girl has for the most part fallen silent, now that it has become clear how completely one can rely on her mental neutrality, her physical neutrality is beginning to manifest itself, and the provocativeness once displayed by this wobbling, uncoordinated yet at the same time reticent piece of flesh appears to have vanished. This body, it appears, is not provocative at all, and there would be little point getting rough with it, as it is sure to offer no resistance whatever, and so any lust directed toward it—lust tempered with aversion, to be sure—will sink into it as if it were made of felt, it will simply be swallowed up, absorbed, suffocated. In retrospect, the boys find their earlier attacks on

the girl's skirt and underpants incomprehensible. This creature, which at first, though unclean, oversized and coarse, was
clearly female, now becomes someone in whose presence the
circles of both male and female intimates alike do not hesitate
to speak without shyness or even premeditation about sexual
matters. They begin to entrust the girl with notes that she is to
deliver to this or that fellow pupil, and unfailingly she returns
with the answer, they teach her special combinations of
knocks by which she is to warn them when a teacher is
approaching, then they station her in front of a dormitory
room, whose door they barricade from the inside using a mop
handle. The first time she stood watch like this, she was frightened out of her wits when someone inside the room began to
whimper and moan as though he were dying, but the girl
stuck to her post, and meanwhile she has gotten used to these
noises and no longer wonders about what sort of pain this is.

Whereas there almost never used to be a seat free when the girl
wanted to do her homework in the common room—usually
she had to sit on the floor with her notebook, which she
endured without complaint—now there is room for her, she
is tolerated by the others, and now and then someone even
asks her a question. The girl always answers either Yes or No.
Questions that cannot be answered with Yes or No she simply

leaves unanswered, she pretends she has to think about the answer, and then continues to think about it until her inter-locutor has forgotten the question. The girl develops a special technique that allows her, even when she is answering only Yes or No, to make her answer as small as possible so as not to cause embarrassment for anyone by her agreement or disagreement, she bends down under the table as if to retrieve some fallen object while saying Yes or saying No, or else she hides her face behind her fists and murmurs into them. She herself asks no questions, not only out of shame, but also because she wouldn't know what questions to ask.

What do you want to be?

The girl is silent.

I don't know what I want to be yet, maybe a veterinarian. But there's still time.

Silence.

The girl sits there in silence, she doesn't bend down under the table as if to retrieve something, she doesn't hide her face behind fists, she just sits there in silence. And while Nancy is going on about the poor whales, the poor lions and the poor rats, the girl's nose begins to run, and it seems to her as if she has lost, along with her memory of what used to be, her memory of what is supposed to be some day. She appears to herself like someone who has been charred into a little ball, someone who has been charred in time as in a fire and is now nothing more than a blackened lump that has been deposited at a home for children.

The girl is very grateful, and though she doesn't speak much in general, she does say Thank you rather frequently, indeed sometimes does so even at moments when others might register complaints or at least voice disagreement. For instance, she says Thank you when one of her classmates, Maik, a lanky boy with a face like a bird, takes her best ballpoint pen away from her with a curt nod, so he can weight his paper airplanes with it. Once, in the middle of a turbulent physics lesson, this Maik had his face slapped by Saskia, a hirsute dark beauty who had been hoping by this act to create a stir—in which she did not succeed. Maik, however, succeeded in this, by slapping Saskia right back, whereupon she began to bawl, and the red spot burning on her left cheek was still visible at recess. It is this story the girl is thinking of when she thanks Maik for taking her best pen away from her. She is saying Thank you for the privilege of knowing him.

The girl's dreams are coming true. It began when Babette, her devout roommate, gave her one of her bracelets, one of those colorful woven bracelets children like to wear. And the girl is no longer excluded when the others make plans in her presence to watch television in the evening or have tea together in the afternoon, they are permitted to make tea in the little kitchen next to the TV room. Often the girl has shown up for these dates and, according to plan, is allowed to take her place beside the others on the threadbare couches in the TV room. Sometimes, though, a date was set, and no one but the girl showed up. They had canceled the gathering without letting her know. Little by little she came to understand that these appointments were made of flimsy stuff, they either took place or they didn't, or they took place tomorrow, or the day thereafter, and word of the cancellation drifted about like a feather. Only because her longing was so cast in stone, her anticipatory pleasure so leaden, had she remained deaf to this light, childish variant of indifference. Little by little it dawned on her that there was no need to feel slighted, these occasions did not go to waste, and childhood was a thing bobbing upon a vast ocean of time. And so if on a Saturday afternoon her roommates should happen to leave the room without saying a word to her in parting, as if the girl did not exist for them, this is in fact the most veritable proof that they accept the girl as one of them. It means that the girl is now as natural a part of the inventory as their lockers and beds. When they start their day in the morning without a word of greeting, this means that there are still many many days lying before them, each indistinguishable from the next, and the faces they will encounter in the morning will be just the same for a very long time, so that it isn't worth making too much of them. One of these faces is the face of the girl.

In the evening, when the girl is already lying in bed with the blanket up to her chin, it now happens from time to time that one of the girls with whom she shares the room comes to sit on the edge of her bed and begins to speak in a low voice. The girl lies on her back with her eyes open, listening. One time it is Nicole, who for reasons beyond her comprehension is hated by the teachers—but that is not what is troubling her, what is troubling her is that she is in love with the mathematics teacher, whom first of all it is forbidden to love, and who secondly is so indifferent to her that of all the teachers he is the only one who doesn't hate her. Another time it is Mandy, the little one, Mandy who is almost as small as a dwarf, for some reason she can't grow any more, but that is not what is troubling her, what is troubling her is that she wants to go home, even though she hadn't even known what a potato was before she arrived at the Home, her mother had never given her a potato to eat. The girl is lying on her back, she has all the time in the world, it would appear, her eyes are open, and all the girls who wish to confide in her can be certain that she will never fall asleep while they are enumerating their woes, nor reveal anything of what she has heard, and from the point of view of those pouring their hearts out, this is highly estimable, comradely behavior. The girl's behavior might remind one a little of the way she stuffs herself with large quantities of food, for here, too, one can behold a silent gluttony which takes in everything, never to release it again, but this similarity does not occur to the others, perhaps because, while they are speaking to the girl, they always turn their backs to her. All these stories tumble down into the girl's cloudy head as if falling down a well, and there they rest.

Among real girlfriends it often happens that one who has let herself go in the presence of the other feels remorse for having told something that would have better been left untold, and now she feels she has sullied herself somehow. For once you have said something that should have been left unsaid, even if only to a girlfriend, you have shouted it out into the world, and even if this girlfriend happens not to pass on the story to anyone else, it still has been shouted into the world, and of course you feel ashamed at not having been able to restrain yourself. But speaking to the girl about these things is a quite different matter. Telling her something isn't like shouting it into the world, it's more like thinking aloud. The girl lets the one who is speaking to her have the entire conversation to herself, she doesn't interrupt, doesn't interject comments of her own, doesn't seize control of the conversation, doesn't use what the other girl has told her as a stirrup to hoist herself into some story of her own, for she has no stories of her own. It is a pure seeing, a disinterested pleasure with which the girl receives these reports, and this explains the other girls' sense that they haven't divulged their secrets to anyone at all when they tell them to her. The girl simply lies there on her back, stringing monologues onto the iron bands that are wrapped around her heart. The others speak, and after a little while the thicket of problems that have been put into words begins to clear and the bit of advice the girl has not given them appears on the horizon of its own accord.

As these nocturnal sessions were just beginning, Nicole in particular, the blond one, worried that it might offend the girl to be spoken to of love, since she herself surely had no hope at all of ever being loved. Of course Nicole herself has just as little hope of ever touching the heart of the mathematics teacher, but this is a fanciful sort of hopelessness, the sort of pain suffered by a girl who is beautiful, a beautiful pain, a blond pain. She has no way of knowing that the girl not only feels no envy, but on the contrary feels that her very existence virtually depends on her ability to keep all contamination of this sort far from her own person, that it is only her own innocence that gives her sojourn here a meaning. Sometimes though, on quite rare occasions, the girl finds herself assailed by knowledge for seconds at a time while her girlfriends, seated on the edge of her bed, are making their confessions before her, it is as if the curtain the girl had sewn shut before her were suddenly being ripped open. At such moments she can no longer close her eyes to the fact that her companions are just in the process of leaving childhood behind them. Her own purity is the only thing that will be able to postpone its decay a short while longer, in this she trusts with the blindness of hope and grants them absolution.

The girl falls down. Early one morning, just before eight, right as she has arrived in front of the school building with the other girls, she slips in a puddle of melted snow and falls down and scrapes her knees. Everyone saw it happen, a few of them laughed, but Nicole, the blond one, helped the girl get up, Nicole took her by one of her huge elbows and pulled her to her feet, found a Band-Aid and placed it on the girl's bloody knee. Like the ribbon of a secret order, this Band-Aid, now hidden beneath long pants, adorns the scraped knee of the girl, and thus corresponds to the many other Band-Aids that adorn many other scraped juvenile knees that are hidden beneath long pants. At night, under the covers with a flash-light, the girl carefully examines her knee and the Band-Aid Nicole has placed over the wound. She isn't surprised at having fallen, for the blood of one who takes up residence in the flesh of a child becomes child's blood, and child's blood is always looking for a way to escape into the open. Children do, in fact, fall down.

After this fall, the girl ceases to menstruate, she is now rid of the unpleasant odor, the nausea and cramps. The longer she succeeded in suppressing the pain during these episodes of indisposition, the more reliably the moment would come when everything went white before her eyes and she had to be escorted by a classmate down to the basement, to the women's lounge, the only room in the orphanage that was always ice-cold. Once it was Nicole who accompanied her downstairs, and once the girl had lain down on the couch, she covered her up, sat down on a chair next to the couch and held her hand. After a while she plucked up courage to ask the girl what it felt like anyhow to have blood running out of you like that, in other words what it felt like to be a real woman. The girl was seized by a sudden fit of nausea and without meaning to she vomited right in Nicole's lap, and although it was only bile, her guilt appeared to her virtually irrevocable, and for the next three days she was unable to look Nicole in the eye.

On Saturdays when many of the others leave the grounds of the Home, whether to visit their parents or, if they are over fourteen years old, to amuse themselves in the city until 8:00 p.m., the girl stays where she is. She doesn't envy any of the ones who leave the grounds, for she knows just how things are on the outside: You stand on a street full of shops with an empty bucket and wait.

On these Saturdays, right after locker inspection, she goes into the day room to see if there is anyone with whom a game of "Aggravation" might be played. If there is no one with whom a game of "Aggravation" might be played, she sits down at one of the formica-topped tables and begins in the especially slow way peculiar to her to write or draw something, anything at all that occurs to her, on scraps of paper she finds lying about. Then she folds up these scraps, puts on her anorak, goes outside and ambles across the muddy grounds. She doesn't even glance at the porter's lodge, which is buzzing with activity since today is visiting day—not out of defiance, she simply forgets to look, she is lost in thought.

The longer she spends in the Home, the better acquainted she becomes with its grounds, and a consequence of this better acquaintance is that she is compelled to move across them more and more slowly if she is to take note of all the particular points with which she is acquainted and savor each one in passing. At first she had seen the back of the kitchen building as a single long wall, but some time later it occurs to her that this back wall has an indentation, a fair-sized niche containing the back entrance to the kitchen, and it is there, in this niche, that the milk delivery service deposits its crates, then the kitchen employees open the door from the inside and drag the crates into the kitchen. So whereas not long ago the girl was just walking along a fifteen-meter wall, she must now, if she is to do the wall justice, also pace the length of this indentation and consider it, she has to look to see whether the milk delivery has arrived, whether the crates are just being dragged into the kitchen, or whether it is snowing on the milk. These and other matters. Sometimes, when no one is watching, she even taps her way along this wall, just to make certain. At the beginning of her sojourn here, the hill that stands at the edge of the grounds appeared to her rather small, but now that she has climbed step by step up one side of it and down the other, she realizes that the hill is in fact possessed of a respectable height and that it is more difficult to climb than was at first apparent. Beads of sweat appeared on the girl's nose even before she reached the top. Now, whenever she walks past this hill, she will no longer be able to dismiss it as a hillock, precisely because she is better acquainted with it, and she will observe it with new eyes and require more time for this observation, she will make a reckoning of the considerable length of time it took her to climb this hill, even if all she is doing now is gazing at it. To be sure, she will climb this hill a few times more, but with ever greater hesitation, and eventually she will cease to climb it at all, and not only because of the unreasonable exertion implied in every act of climbing. The concentration alone is enough to sap her strength: concentrating on the phenomenon that beneath her feet the mountain is, as it were, beginning to grow, that it is practically swelling beneath her as the girl makes her way up its vault. Eventually she will begin merely to stand there for a while at the foot of the mountain, observing or, whenever possible, touching a handful of earth that has been piled up or a trace in the mud in which melted snow has collected, and she will find an entire landscape in this little heap of earth, this muddy furrow. Static observation of this sort is a worthy substitute, she finds, for the tiring walk.

Did you grow up on the moon? they used to ask her during gym class, for they found it beyond comprehension that the girl didn't know any of the rules for the various ball games commonly played by children, and so the teams with hopes of winning feared and shunned her. She was, however, still capable of jumping—little jumps, but still jumps all the same, awkward lunges to the right or left by which nothing was achieved, but they did give the impression that the girl was at least trying to participate in the game in some mean-ingful way. Meanwhile she has learned to keep the rules for basketball, volleyball and dodgeball in her head, but she now also knows that there are hundreds of possibilities for doing something wrong. This knowledge robs her movement of that slight bit of élan it had formerly possessed. A rigidness over-comes the girl, like a great fleshy block she stands there on the playing field between her smooth-skinned, agile classmates, she is afraid of the ball, and her ability to at least get out of its way is in constant decline. Then it happens, the ball flies directly into her arms which she is holding crossed over her chest, and before she even knows how this has occurred, she is clutching this terrifying ball, clutching it and clutching it as if rooted to the spot, and the others are shouting, and the girl listens to all these shouts crisscrossing back and forth beneath the roof of the gymnasium.

Jenny Erpenbeck

Now it is still dark outside when the wake-up call comes. The instructor on duty bangs on the door from the outside, and a moment later, on his way back down the corridor, he pulls it open a crack, reaches inside and turns on the neon lights. The girl's three roommates are tossing in their beds, their eyes still closed. The rules thrust themselves right in the middle of their dreams, and the first thought to follow upon the dream is, without fail, the thought of the test that day in school, every day there is a test, not a single day passes all winter long without there being a test on something or other, the moment you put a toe out of bed you're already in the jaws of the test. Their hearts full of reluctance, these nymphs arise, slip barefoot into their crushed slippers and shuffle out of the room and down the hall to the washroom, where they brush their white teeth. The girl envies them the matter-of-factness of their displeasure, these clearly defined battle lines, the absoluteness of their ill humor, these children's indisputable right to feel defiance.

The girl herself is already lying there with her eyes open long before the first bang on the door, she is already awake, lying there with the covers pulled up to her chin while the other three sleep on, she does not stir, she just watches. Her eyes have become used to the darkness, and thus she observes the three others as they lie in their beds. They lie there in disorder, the covers clamped between their legs, saliva running out of their open mouths onto their pillows, they have gotten lost in sleep, Mandy, the dwarf, is counting in her sleep, millions upon millions she counts, the two others are quiet, Nicole is sleeping with her eyes half open, but this is only a physical defect, the girl has confirmed this: one night she crept up to Nicole's bed and held her hand before Nicole's half-open eyes without anything happening. The cross that Babette wears on a leather cord around her neck is now imprinting itself on her throat, it is squeezed in between her throat and the pillow. None of the three sleepers knows that the time allotted for sleeping will soon be at an end, for they are still surrounded by dreams, but the girl knows that in just a moment there will be a bang on the door. It is much more awful to know this than it is to be torn from one's slumber by a bang on the door.

On the thirteenth of February, the city was fire-bombed for the first time, it was bombed once, and then, as people were just beginning to creep out of the air-raid cellars, a second time, it was bombed so hard that the river on which the city lies began to boil, and of the city itself nothing was left. Now that so many years have passed since the bombing, the city exists again, and there is a home for children in it, and all the children have been called to assembly because the director wishes to make a speech. It is afternoon, the children are seated in the dining hall, the tables today are covered with white cloths, upon each table stands a burning candle and a plate of cake, but the cake may not be eaten until the director has finished his speech. The girl sees the white-clad tables and the candles, but above all she sees the cake, and eagerly anticipates the end of the speech. She listens carefully to what the director is saying, so as not to miss the end of the speech, and she has her eye on the largest piece of cake. But then something happens that has never before happened: The girl loses her appetite, at precisely the point in the speech when the director is telling about the boiling river, and how the people who tried to leap into the river to escape the flames were boiled alive. Maik gives a whoop, and Björn rubs his stomach in imitation of a cannibal, but the girl loses every last bit of appetite, carefully she gets up from the table and without a word, by pressing the palms of her hands together, asks those seated around her to move their chairs to let her through. She goes into the kitchen, sits down on one of the stools and remains there, gazing at the enormous rump of one of the cooks who is leaning out through the hatch to hear the director's speech. She asks the back of the cook: Why is there a birthday party when the people were boiled alive? She asks hesitantly, but the cook heard her clearly, as though the question were made of different stuff than air and had brushed against her body. She turns around to face the girl, like someone waking up from a deep sleep, and says: You have to celebrate what you cannot forget.

Some days the girl doesn't comb her hair and is very quiet, quieter even than usual, and so tired that she falls asleep in the middle of a lesson. The teachers do not notice because the girl props her head in her hands as though she were thinking, a technique she has learned from observing her classmates. On one such day, Nicole walked up to the girl during recess and asked if she were sad. She even tried to put her arm around the girl, but this was awkward because the girl's shoulders are so broad, and so she took her arm back down again. All the girl said was that she wanted to sleep, she was so tired, so very very tired. Nicole didn't believe her, she raised her index finger and said: You mustn't be sad! And since the girl never does anything she isn't allowed to, she at once began to smile.

There is a secret meeting place, a shed whose lock is broken. Only rarely does the custodian come to fetch something from this shed: rakes when leaves have fallen, snow shovels when there is snow. And when he has raked the leaves or shoveled the snow, he returns the tools to the shed and hangs the lock in its place as though it would lock, but it doesn't lock any more. Often the girl had wondered where her classmates disappeared to after school, she'd kept her eyes open during her slow circuits across the grounds, and only rarely encountered one of them. But recently her classmates have stopped making an effort to conceal their meeting place from the girl. Her taciturnity has caused her to increase in value, in other words, she isn't seen as a nuisance. When she pushes open the door to the shed, the others no longer even turn around. She is allowed to join them, to sit down at the edge of the circle of secret smokers of both sexes, and, when she gets cold, to leave again, with neither her arrival nor her departure prompting anyone to question her. Once Saskia even offers her a cigarette, but the girl refuses it. Grandmother, then why do you have such yellow teeth? Saskia shrieks, and leans far back so as to show off what a large bosom she has already. Her intention is not to insult the girl, and this the girl knows. She is used to being used, to being taken by the shoulders and spun around, bent over or having her knees pressed forward to demonstrate a dance step or a game or something else, she knows she is well suited to providing an occasion for laughter that is so loud that all eyes fall upon the one who is laughing, not on the laughter's object. It is in just such a way that Saskia makes her joke about the girl, without genuinely wishing to subject her to ridicule—rather, her objective is to attract the attention of the boy standing next to her. It is Maik with the bird face, the one with whom she recently traded slaps, he is the one who's supposed to laugh, but he doesn't laugh, just continues to smoke and blow out the smoke through his nostrils and follow it with his eyes as it vanishes in the semi-darkness between rakes and snow shovels. Saskia gazes up at him the way women gaze up at a man, but Maik continues to look straight in front of him, the way men look straight in front of them when a woman is gazing up at them. The grandmother with the yellow teeth is standing near the circle, just outside it, for the moment she has been forgotten again, and thus she feels at ease. Outside a storm is raging, but inside this shed there is no wind.

Once the girl came into the shed, the sun had already set, she just wanted to have a glance to see if there wasn't someone there, noiselessly she entered since it is her nature to enter noiselessly, and at once she realized that something was wrong. She stopped just inside the door, and stood there in the shadows peering into the back part of the shed, which was lit by the orange rays of a streetlamp that came through the row of tiny windows just under the roof. The two boys in the shed didn't notice the girl entering because she didn't make a sound. She remained standing there and saw the two boys, one of them lying on a stack of hardened cement sacks, the other squatting beside him. She hadn't been able to understand what was happening and therefore, out of curiosity, remained standing there. The one who was lying down has opened his pants, and a newspaper conceals his upper body. The one squatting next to him has taken the penis of his companion in his ink-stained hand and is rubbing it. At the same time, he is speaking, he has a speech impediment and speaks with a lisp. He lisps: It's Nicole, your Nicole, kiss me, Dennis, it's Nicole, your Nicole, I've been waiting so long for you. Both boys are breathing quickly, expelling their breath in white clouds, it is cold. The one who is squatting rubs his friend's penis harder. He lisps: Let me show you my breasts, Dennis, it's Nicole, your Nicole, touch me, touch me between my legs, I'm already all wet, Dennis, Dennis, I want you to put it in me, put it in me Dennis, put it in me. The boy lying down moans and clutches at his friend, the semen spurts out of his penis and rains down on the newspaper, the girl hears the pattering sound it makes and leaves the shed. She walks for a little down the avenue of poplars, then stops short, takes hold of one of the poplars, bends down to the edge of the road and vomits up everything she has inside her.

No pain, no gain, the gym teacher had said. Meanwhile the girl's weakness goes far beyond gym class. There is the exertion of bending down from one's chair to take a book out of one's book bag, or the impossibility of answering in a loud enough voice a question asked by someone standing twenty meters away. For a while—as once when everyone began chanting in unison to urge on a fight—it had even seemed to her that her voice had grown stronger. But now she has stopped trying to fool herself. She had confused her own voice with the voice of the group, had thought she was shouting at the top of her lungs, whereas in fact almost no sound at all had come from her open mouth. When she is sitting on her perch in the twilight, she can see from a distance how Maik, Björn and the others are playing soccer, how they run about shooting goals of their own free will until dark, while she herself has to be happy she still has the strength to hoist her body up to this bar on which she so likes to perch. Inwardly she is tormented by a sentence that someone she can no longer recall said to her a long, long time ago: Everything you build up with your hands you knock down again with your rear end. Perhaps this is the source of the difficulty she has moving at all. The girl used to be constantly looking around to the right and left to be sure of doing whatever the right thing was, but now that she can see more clearly and perceives the great variety of human beings moving all around her in a thousand different ways, she can no longer choose what is right, she no longer knows what the right thing is. Everything she does seems to her wrong even while she is doing it, so utterly wrong that she'd like to take it back again——never would she have wished to give offense to anyone, but now she is forced to realize that there is virtually no action at all that is free of the possibility of causing offense. At the same time, this state of being prevented from acting cannot merely be described as a lack of independence, as is so often done by the girl's teachers with pedagogical intent, it is more like a paralysis. Even transforming a simple thought into action, such as, for example, wanting to lift one's hand, is becoming more and more impossible for the girl the longer she remains in the institution. If you lift your hand, you must, a moment before, have wanted to lift your hand, if you laugh, you must have wanted to laugh, if you say no or yes, you must have wanted to say no or yes, in other words every time you do something, you must have wanted, a moment earlier, to do what you are doing. The moment you do anything at all, your volition can be seen standing naked behind it, and this the girl finds so utterly embarrassing that she chooses to want nothing. She wants what all the others want, but there is no such thing. And the moment she realizes this, she realizes also that her strength is waning.

The snow has turned gray, turned black and melted, and now there are great puddles everywhere. Then the sun begins to shine. The girl sits down in the empty day room on the first warm Saturday, when all the others have gone off together on some weekend outing, and writes a letter, a short letter on a scrap of paper, she writes extremely slowly, as is her habit, one capital letter after the other, like a faucet dripping, each letter stands there in isolation, unconnected to its neighbors. The girl folds the paper and writes in large letters on the outside: TO ME. Then she gets up from the formica-topped table on which she has been writing and pulls on her anorak. She stuffs the letter inside the anorak, next to her heart, and goes out into the sunshine. She places one foot after the other. She strolls across the grounds to the animal cemetery Nancy has secretly established for the poor rats, the poor mice, the poor little birds, strolls to where the little wooden crosses are standing, crosses on which are scratched the fantastical names Nancy bestowed on these creatures in honor of their deaths. Next to the animal cemetery she mails her letter, she bends down and inserts it between the boards of an old fruit crate that stands rotting upside-down beside a grave marked with a brick. This grave is the final resting place of the pigeon Kamikaze. The girl knows the story. Flying at top speed, the pigeon crashed into the window of Nancy's room one morning, then dropped to the ground, its neck broken.

The letter falls into the phosphorescent semi-darkness, joining all the other letters addressed TO ME. These letters, if anyone were ever to find and unfold them, would be full of sand, and it would no longer be possible to read all the words without effort, they are faded and smeared because snow has so often fallen upon the crate, or else rain, some of them are in fact entirely bleached out and are no longer anything more than folded dirty-white sheets of paper. But no one finds these letters, no one unfolds them, and no one makes the effort to read them.

One of them says: BE NICE, OR ELSE YOU'LL BE STRUCK DEAD. BEST WISHES—YOUR MAMA.

Another one: NEVER GO OUT IN THE DARK AGAIN WITHOUT YOUR CAP, OR ELSE THE CROWS WILL PECK YOUR EYES OUT. BEST WISHES—YOUR MAMA. This letter contains a sketch in which one can see seven dark birds flying toward the viewer bearing umbrellas, the flock is so dense there is scarcely any room left for the sky between them. The sketch is subtitled: THE BRETHREN. But now this inscription is blurred, and the sketch itself has faded beyond recognition.

DON'T STICK YOUR HEAD SO FAR OUT THE WINDOW, OR ELSE IT MIGHT FALL OFF. BEST WISHES—YOUR MAMA is one of the better-preserved letters. This one, too, contains a sketch, one that shows someone putting his head through an open window, but the upper edge of the window frame is serrated like the blade of a knife, and there is an arrow leading straight down from it to the neck of the one who is sticking his head out. Beneath this sketch stand the words: I AM TOO CURIOUS.

Another letter consists only of a sketch. It shows a very fat person, whether man or woman is impossible to say, perhaps it is supposed to be a snowman, for the creature is made of three spheres piled one atop the other, though the row of buttons is missing, the carrot and broom. This person has been marked invalid with two long crisscrossing lines. Underneath is written: HUNGER AND THIRST. The figure itself can scarcely be recognized any longer, but the two lines crossing it out are perfectly clear, and the subtitle has run in the dampness but remains legible.

The letter the girl mailed today reads: AS FAR AS I'M CONCERNED, YOU ARE DEAD. BEST WISHES—YOUR MAMA. Here, as in all the other letters, not a single written character contains a curve: the D has not a belly but four corners, the S is not a snake but a lightning flash, and the O is an empty square. The letters look as if they have been carved in stone, but the weather will eat away at them, just as it has eaten away at the other scraps of paper.

Early the next morning the girl is lying in bed preparing herself for the moment when the bang on the door will come. Then the bang on the door comes. The girl wants to get up, but she cannot get up. Her legs seem to her as heavy as if they were frozen. Then she begins to cry. The three others come over to her bed, drowsy and barefoot, and ask what the matter is, but the girl cannot explain herself. So get up then! The girl can't. Nicole kneels down beside her bed and doesn't know what to say. She gazes into this large, blotchy face, mute now, that is turned toward her, and it is like looking at the surface of an unknown planet. She is afraid of this immobile mass, and at the same time ashamed of her fear. The girl has let her head sink back into the pillows and has stopped moving. The only thing about her that is in motion is her nose, which is running. Nicole pulls a tissue out of the sleeve of her nightgown and wipes the girl's nose clean. The girl thanks her.

Then they come for her. She is lifted onto a stretcher and transported to the infirmary where she'd had to spend so much time upon her arrival at the Home. Recently she had been healthier. Slower, but healthier. Now she has a six-bed room all to herself, for no one else would think of falling ill in the springtime. Early on, she has them lift her a few times into a wheelchair and then rides—shouting with pleasure, to everyone's surprise—up and down the corridor at great speed. Then she quiets down, stays in bed all day, and then another day, and then another, waiting for visitors. She thinks the others can't come to visit her because they have to prepare for the big chemistry project. The day of the chemistry project passes, and then another day, and then another, and no one comes. Cast out of time, the girl lies in her hospital bed, but the face presented by each of the weekdays remains distinct in her memory. She can still remember with meticulous precision the structure of each individual weekday, right on schedule she feels precisely those feelings which she felt on each of these days when she still went to school, and thus she maintains her connection to her young friends. Thank goodness there's a clock in her infirmary room, so she always knows what feeling is in order. Even if she cannot move, she still keeps an eye on this clock.

And so on Monday from eight o'clock until nine thirty-five she feels English, with a little break in the middle. Then there is a feeling for the recess period. From nine fifty-five until ten forty she feels chemistry, and afterward, from ten forty-five until eleven thirty, biology. Recess feeling. Finally, starting at eleven fifty, she is overtaken by the exhaustion that always came over her during gym class. At twelve thirty-five on the dot she heaves a sigh of relief, the way all children sigh in relief day after day when school lets out. You might think all these minutes, hours and days the girl experiences chained to her bed were new, unprecedented. But this isn't true, they aren't new, in fact they wouldn't even be there at all if they hadn't already existed, once, in the era of the girl's happiness. In this way, Tuesday doesn't follow a Monday, but rather derives all its force from the fact that it is a Tuesday, week after week always a Tuesday—recognizable by a certain succession of school subjects and recess breaks. Although it is physically impossible for the girl to return to the scene of her crime, memory teaches her to stutter.

After school, after the precisely timed sigh of relief, the girl generally falls asleep, for she had never been able to achieve absolute certainty regarding the face worn by time at the end of the school day, the face of free time, she doesn't know whether to be happy or tense or indifferent or filled with nausea if she wishes to resurrect it. This had been a time of a thousand faces, one that resisted every form of planning, varying according to the weather, homework assignments, the promise of amusements, and sometimes it simply remained a mystery and the girl wasn't even able to learn what was going on. For this reason she now—i.e., starting Mondays at twelve thirty-five, Tuesdays at one twenty-five, Wednesdays also at one twenty-five, Thursdays not until two thirty, and Fridays already at eleven thirty—has nothing to hold on to. Therefore she spends this time sleeping. Her sleep is interrupted only for meals, which take place at the same times as for the others on the outside: tea and cake at three o'clock, dinner at six. Only in this way can she make herself believe everything is holding its breath and remains familiar to her. The girl doesn't look out the window, before which the trees are gradually unfolding their green. In her head it is snowing and snowing.

Once she wakes up at ten after eight on a Thursday, she's slept through the beginning of the first period: the beginning of gym class. The others have already lined up, perhaps they've even begun the day's first races. For one brief moment, the girl's lame body is filled with warmth, the warmth of terror at having overslept. She doesn't understand how she could have done this, since the patients in the infirmary are woken at six. Every one of these winter Thursdays had begun with gym class at dawn. The sun would rise during their endurance run. Today, though, the sun is refusing to rise. Something is wrong. When the nurse comes in, bringing the tea for the night, the girl realizes that she mistook the time of day. It isn't morning at all, it's evening. She has bumped up against time like a blind person, at this she has to weep. And the hand she always used to blow her nose with is as heavy as lead, she cannot lift it.

The girl dreads the arrival of the first weekend, for she has no collective feeling, one common to her and all the others, for how a weekend should proceed. On weekends the pupils were always scattered to the winds, the fourteen-year-olds were driven into the arms of their parents and various amusements, which the girl neither knew nor wished to know. She wouldn't have had any notion what to feel on these infinitely long two days if there hadn't at least been locker inspection. As a shipwrecked sailor clings to a tiny bit of wood that is floating in the vastness of the ocean, the girl holds fast to her memory of locker inspection. On Saturdays early in the afternoon is when this general ransacking and purging of items that had not, in the opinion of the instructor on duty, been suitably stacked, occurred, a ritual which as such does not interest the girl at the moment—the little "s", though, that's the main thing, the little "s" at the end of the word "Saturdays", modest as it is, this "s", it consoles her. This "s" stands for order and discipline, it signifies that one knows what to do and what not to do, and in general that one knows how things stand. This "s" is the short but splendid tail gracing all these days the girl has been able to preserve in her memory: Mondays, Tuesdays, Wednesdays, Thursdays, Fridays and Saturdays—it sheds light on the girl's logical fallacy: mistaking what was for what is.

But all the long Sunday she spends exiled to her bed, the girl feels she might starve to death. On Sunday, too, no one comes to visit her.

In the end, the girl stops waiting, she tells herself that it is perhaps even a good sign that none of these children is willing to view her massive, breathing cadaver. She believes she recognizes in the absence of her fellow pupils that same healthy indifference she had noticed before when they neglected to take leave of her or when an appointment had been cancelled, an indifference she had come to respect. What she doesn't know is that the indifference the others now display with regard to her is more thorough than originally intended. At first, for example, Nicole was definitely planning to drop by the infirmary, but each time she was about to, something or other would come up, until finally she had to admit to herself that she felt a certain aversion—quite a strong one, in fact—to the idea of visiting the girl. A large, long sigh of relief sweeps through the classroom when it is announced that the girl's absence is expected to last for quite some time. While others who fall ill or have to leave the Home remain a topic of conversation for days and weeks on end, while everyone wants to know whether, in the one case, they are in pain or have to be operated on, or in the other, where they have gone to and what the reason was for their departure, even if they were only temporary residents of the Home—the girl's whereabouts, by contrast, are never discussed. This silence is all the more remarkable as it seems poorly suited to the position the girl had formerly occupied. It is too great a silence. It speaks of an extraordinary, indelible wrong. But neither Maik with the bird face, nor Nicole, nor Erik, the neighbor with technical aptitude, not even Björn or Saskia—no one would be able to say what it is the girl has done to make everyone erase her with their silence. But within them blossoms a great, monstrous hope: that she might never return.

The doctors, in an unguarded moment, referred to the girl's body as a bag of bones, and this figure of speech pursues her into sleep, she is compelled again to dream: of elbows slipping out of place, and of a skull so heavy it slides down beneath the skin until it rests between her knees, of ulcerous wounds, exposed sinews that have grown twisted together so that it is necessary to take a knife and slice through them.

Not once since arriving at the Home for Children has the girl left its grounds. Nothing in the world could have moved her to walk out through the gate of her own free will, even for a moment, and she took part in none of the popular group outings or class trips. But now it has come to this, the doctors, *horribile dictu*, are at their wits' end. We've done all we can do, they say, having completed all the examinations that can be carried out in the infirmary of a children's home, and they decide to send the girl to the General Municipal Hospital for a more thorough evaluation. As the orderly is hoisting the girl from her bed to the litter, she says: Over my dead body! The orderly shrugs: Whatever you say.

In the Municipal Hospital, the girl is brought to the children's ward, but above and below, to the right and the left of the children's ward, lie the adults, breathing. And every afternoon between two and five are visiting hours, and the ward fills up with people from the city, it fills with mothers and fathers, with flowers and cake. Every day between two and five, the girl buries her face in her pillow.

Thanks to the strict diet, something happens that no one would have thought possible: the girl becomes thin. All over her body, the now superfluous skin begins to droop in folds, and her face takes shape in a monstrous way: It is becoming the face of an adult. The doctors in the children's ward are the first to notice. Shaking their heads in disbelief, they appear again and again at the girl's bedside, and soon even the doctors from other wards come to join the group of those whose scientific curiosity has gotten the better of them. They observe the progress of this development and discuss among themselves how such a monstrous transformation could be possible. It is as if the excitement and hubbub generated by the girl's case, along with the struggle to comprehend what in fact the girl is, are increasing at just the same rate at which the girl is becoming, from each day to the next, sleepier and sleepier, scarcely does she so much as open her eyes any longer to distinguish all the many lab-coated persons who again and again assemble at her bedside, scarcely does she listen any longer to the diagnostic murmurings when various theories regarding her illness are proposed, discussed and rejected in front of her, as if she were still nothing more than a child. Within a period of perhaps two weeks, this face that, rough or coarse as it may have been, was still once decidedly childish, appears to recede, and in its place the features of a woman emerge, as if the illness were an artist who at last had succeeded in releasing the form once imprisoned in the stone. As if out of a general consensus that there must be something indecent about so unnatural an aging process, the girl in the end is summarily rolled bed and all into a single room, far from the eyes of the children with whom she had been sharing a ward.

But the girl does not continue to age and turn gray prematurely as happens with those children who are born old, whose illness is well-known and has been studied, rather she ceases to age after approximately two weeks, when she has come to resemble a woman of thirty. And just as every realization reaches us in a state of increasing acceleration, just as every insight comes crashing down like an avalanche, that is, at first nothing at all happens, but then, at who knows what point in time and for what reason, the realization begins, and eventually, once the necessary courage has been mustered to consider possible the impossible, it becomes a force that cannot be held back by anyone or anything any longer—it is in just such a way that the process of realizing who the girl really is unfolds. Whether it was that even when the girl was still lying in the children's ward one of the visitors from the city recognized her emerging face, or that the doctors examined the girl's bone substance the way one might count the rings of a tree and then passed on the results, and that the police then began to search for the girl's face among their missing persons reports and not, as before, when the girl had turned up with her bucket, among the files of missing children—perhaps several of these things occurred simultaneously. In any case what was previously perceived as a genuine existence now is seen to have been a calculated deception, a masquerade and nothing more. The girl, who is no longer a girl, has laid aside her costume, her own skin, and before everyone's eyes has put an end to this carnival performance, as if her childhood were nothing but a joke, as if it had been given her to stroll up and down in time as in a garden, and in this attitude, despite all the modesty the girl displayed as a child and now continues to display unchanged, there is something offensive, something arrogant, a certain contempt for the natural course of things, even a challenge to God. This feeling is shared among all the members of the lab-coated audience who witnessed this inexplicable masquerade, but no one speaks of it. It is with satisfaction, such as that with which one might receive a long-overdue offering, that it is reported how often the patient is now seen to weep, she weeps even when her eyes are closed, in sleep, her prank has flopped, her attempt to stop time in its tracks has failed.

On Wednesday the doctor escorts a gray-haired old lady into the hospital room. Through the bars over the windows, which have been flung wide open, the smell of lilac floats into the room. The old lady is exhausted. Shame is written all over her face. The doctor pushes her closer to the bed. Here we are, he says to the woman lying immobile in the bed, this is your mother. The mother is silent. Oh, are you my mother? says the woman who used to be the girl, and very slowly she opens her eyes. I don't remember you at all.

The Book of Words

For my father,
with all my heart

'Usually all that's left is a few bones.'
Schimmeck

'An entire generation vanished here.'
Fonderbrider

'... bên zi bêna, bluot zi bluoda
lid zi geliden, sôse gelîmida sîn!

... bone to bone, blood to blood
limb to limbs, thus be they bonded.'
2nd Merseburg Incantation

What are my eyes for if they can see but see nothing? What are my ears for if they can hear but hear nothing? Why all this strangeness inside my head?

All of it must be thought into nothingness, one whorl of gray matter at a time, until in the end a spoonful of me will be left glistening at the bottom. I must seize memory like a knife and turn it against itself, stabbing memory with memory. If I can.

Father and mother. Ball. Car. These might be the only words that were still intact when I learned them. Then even they got turned around, ripped out of me and stuck back in upside-down, making the opposite of ball ball, the opposite of father and mother father and mother. What is a car? All the other words had silent halves dragging them down from the start like lead weights around ankles, just as the moon lugs its dark half around with it even when it's full. But it keeps circling in its orbit all the same. For me, words used to be stable, fixed in place, but now I'm letting them all go, if need be I'll cut off a foot if that's the only way to get rid of them. Ball. Ball.

Lullaby and goodnight. My mother is putting me to bed. She strokes my head as she sings. White, dry hand stroking the head of a child. *With roses bedight.* Eyes the color of water gazing at me; already my eyelids are falling shut. *With lilies o'erspread*, she sings. But lilies are for funerals. Not these lilies, she'd say if she saw the words were making me cry again, they aren't real lilies at all, they're just lilies-of-the-valley for faeries to sleep under. But tonight it's already too late for crying, I've traveled too far into the land of sleep to turn around, and they aren't lilies-of-the valley, they're real lilies that someone I don't know is going to lay on my coffin and nail it shut as I sleep. *Lay thee down now and rest*, she sings. She pulls the blanket up to my chin and turns out the light. The coffin nails scrape my skin, lots of little bloody wounds. *May thy slumbers be blessed.* And what if they aren't blessed? Then I'll remain lying here in my coffin-bed forever. *May thy slumbers be blessed.* And the drops of blood will turn to stone. Mother.

A ball is a thing that rolls and sometimes bounces. A father is a man who stays taller than you for a long time. Before my father goes to confession, he shaves and puts on a clean shirt. If a person wanted to play ball with someone's head, only the nose would get in the way. Before my father goes to confession, he takes me on his lap and lets me ride his knees. Many, many children have already ridden into this landscape and become fodder for ravens, countless white-skinned screeching riders who never seem to manage a full gallop before they've tumbled down into the bog between their fathers' knees. My father's shirt smells fresh and is rough when I bury my head in it after I've pulled myself up out of the bog with a motion that makes me dizzy every time. Father.

House. Our house is the exact center of the garden. Pink walls, the pink bleached by the sun and already flaking. I slip a fingernail beneath the plaster and snap it off. Underneath, an ocher color comes to light. When I tap a rock against this hidden paint, yet another layer of skin appears in the islands that result: gray. I can't go any deeper than this, the gray clings firmly to the walls of the house, perhaps this gray really is the house itself. My mother says: Stop that. I know, I know: If I want to go into the house, I can use the front door.

From sunshine to shade. Naked soles padding from the dust outside to the cool stone. Barefoot. The sun is almost always shining here, it shines and shines and shines, and the sky around the sun is almost always completely empty. What does the sun eat? I ask my father. Water, he replies. And where is its bed? The sun doesn't sleep, he says. When it is nighttime here, he says, the sun is shining on the other side of the world. Lovely weather today. Today and every day.

Why didn't you have any milk for me, I ask my mother. Some women have a lot of milk, and others none at all, my mother replies. I can remember my wet-nurse's breasts quite clearly. I drank from them for a long time. Longer than any other child I know, my mother says. Even after I started school, the first thing I would do when I came home was sit down on my nurse's lap and drink. Her milk was watery and sweet, her breasts rosy and full, firm islands on the body of an aging woman. My wet-nurse—who even after I had stopped drinking from her held my entire childhood in her lap like an apple—resembled a faerie with green, slanting eyes, one who had been cast out of a faerie tale and now appeared rather somber, thanks to her hair, which had grown darker at the roots and then turned gray, and the colors she wore even in the hottest summer, autumnal hues: brown, black and olive green. To what I saw, I added an invisible, pointed, cone-shaped hat, light blue with a veil. That's just not normal, my mother had said once as she watched me drink from the faerie breasts, and she'd tried to dismiss my wet-nurse. For three entire days I refused to speak, and on the fourth the nurse returned. Milk. Drink.

I never saw my wet-nurse's garden. I don't know whether the shoebox with the hands fell on the grass or into a flowerbed. It doesn't matter, my wet-nurse says to me when I drop my ice cream; she buys me another one. Where my fallen ice cream is melting in the sun, it leaves a bright splotch on the asphalt. Marie, my wet-nurse's daughter, has much longer fingers than I do and never drops her ice cream. And her hands are always clean, no matter what dirty things she touches. My hands are always exactly as sticky and dusty as the things we play with and eat, or as the city streets we fall down on when we're running or push and shove one another. As if her skin were different, though when I take Marie's hand—Marie who is in a matter of speaking my milk-sister—her skin feels just like mine. As if it were actually made of wax or stone so the dirt slides right off. *Our Father, who art in Heaven.* At night when I am lying alone in bed, I creep all the way under the covers and fold my hands, which I have rubbed clean with an eraser to make them just like Marie's; by praying, I am now drawing all of Heaven down into the dark with me, including Our Father. Say good morning, shake hands, shake hands.

Those who, and then their friends, then the ones who remember them, then all who are afraid, and finally everyone. My father says these words behind a closed door in our house, at the time the door still looks huge to me, I imagine what would happen if it were to fall on me while I am pressed against it, listening, wonder whether I'd be crushed flat, through the door the smell of tobacco is filtering into the hall—everyone—and whether it would make a noise when it fell on me, or whether a door like that falls quietly upon a body made of flesh. The next day, hopping from island to island across the city's stone carpet patterns, holding my mother's hand, I count off silently: Those who. Then their friends. The ones who remember. Who are afraid. And finally everyone. Either always the black stones or always the white ones or always the gray, holding my mother's hand. This sentence is like a counting-out rhyme, and like a counting-out rhyme it cannot stop until it reaches the end—I can't interrupt my hopping in the middle, can't just freeze on one leg somewhere in the city, standing on black or white or gray. I am afraid for my father. Everyone. Everyone everyone.

A bird was walking here, my father says. Squatting down beside me, he points out the star-shaped scratches in the dark soil at the edge of our garden, in the shade of the trees where no grass grows. *There were three ravens sat on a tree.* What is a track, I ask my father. A trace that is left behind, something that cannot be caused by chance, my father replies. *They were as black as black might be.* But then before you can know what cannot be caused by chance, I say, you have to know everything else. Probably, my father says. And what about the double time a track like this has. What double time, my father says. The time, I say, when the bird was walking here, and then the second time, when we see it was here—the track is a sort of bridge between them. Perhaps, my father says. But by the time you're finally old enough to tell the difference between chance and everything else, you're too heavy to walk across the bridge. No, my father says, that's silly, and he picks up a little stick and starts making star-shaped scratches beside the star-shaped scratches.

Day after day, my father works in a palace whose exterior is perfectly white. In this palace my father sees to it that things are orderly. Wailing sirens, flashing lights. White walls, white columns, white front steps, blinding sun gleaming off the building as if the building itself were the sun, only the trees to the right and left of it are dark, and there is never a wind stirring their leaves. Wailing, flashing. I wonder whether the windows are just painted on, since the palace always stands there so quietly, my mother says, everything inside it is orderly and well looked after, my father keeps everything in order, and I never see anyone at the windows. It might well be that the building's been walled up, that's why its exterior gleams like that, sunlight cannot enter and get lost inside. Flashing lights. Just as my mother looks after me. Do you comb order, do you give order something to eat and drink? In a building which no light ever enters, in which you have to hold on to the walls and feel your way about because all the windows have been bricked up. More wailing. If you can't find order in the dark, might you accidentally comb the air instead of it, or upset the food and drink, and does the order remain there all the same: dirty, uncombed, ravenous and running wild? Wails upon wails, an explosion of lights. My father comes out of the building, thank goodness, he's holding one hand to his eyes because at first the sun blinds him, but then he sees us, my mother and me, standing at the foot of the steps, it's Friday at half past two, we're picking him up from work as we do every Friday, he runs quickly down the steps and kisses me with his lips that are as soft as a woman's. My father never wears a uniform, and the cars lined up before the building are gray and white, no flashing lights anywhere. Where have the sirens gone wailing off to? They turned into birds, my wet-nurse says. It is sunny and quiet in the middle of our city where the police live.

A miracle, my mother says and points at two black-clad, billowing angels who, hand in hand far off in the distance, are plummeting from the sky above the ocean, the sky is blue, utterly blue, just as blue as the water in which it is mirrored, the angels are plunging from blue to blue, from sky to water, plunging black against the blue with their arms spread wide, holding one another's hands, my mother and I are standing down below at the harbor observing this miracle, and many other people are standing there as well, pointing at the angels and crossing themselves. Red, green and yellow, us on the ground. Orange. The wind slips beneath the angels' clothes, white, white wind, only the clothing of these angels is black, why black, I ask my mother. Black. Black isn't a color.

Or does black come about because you've thrown all the colors together in a single pot. I am sitting on the living room rug, cutting animals I like out of magazines while my mother is off in the kitchen washing lettuce, stirring and chopping, and my father is squatting beside me on the rug holding the paper taut and saying things like: Careful, watch the ears. It's always evening when my father sits beside me on the rug, sometimes even nighttime. When I look up at his head, which I have to look up to see even when he's squatting beside me, that's how tall he is, it appears framed, evening after evening, in the dark rectangle of the uncurtained window behind him. Shiny smooth blackness, no moonlight, and before it this head belonging to my father, which looks light by contrast: blond, light-brown eyes, and teeth like pearls when he opens his mouth and says what is in the pictures. Is it true that a vulture can seize a entire live lamb and carry it up to the sky and then drop it somewhere to eat it? Of course not, my father says, a vulture only eats things that are already dead. He strokes my head while I am cutting out the little lamb. Dinner's ready, my mother calls, we get up and suddenly the entire living room is reflected in that same window and the blackness vanishes. But behind the reflection it is still there, this impenetrable blackness, I know this because the garden, which lies on the other side of the window, is hidden from view all night long. The window has captured the garden and won't let it out, it's thrown a black cloth over it and now is trying to trick us with the colorful reflection of our living room.

In the morning the garden has returned to view, I could probably even walk around in it if I didn't have to go to school;

trees and flowers have been released from captivity, someone has pulled off the black cloth, folded it up and hidden it away somewhere, but only temporarily, until night falls once more, this much is certain. Morning after morning the skirt, knee-highs and shoes in blue, and the shirt with short or long sleeves, white. Just like the others. For years on end, morning after morning: the blue cap on my head, a folded ship made of felt, upside-down as if capsized and fixed in place with a bobby pin, a gold insignia on one side. In the grass the dew glistens, my feet would get cold and damp now if I went outside barefoot, instead I slip into my shoes and lay the scarf, the same blue as the cap, around my neck and tie the knot, a knot that makes the knot itself invisible, my father taught it to me years ago, even before I started school. Blue the sky was, utterly and perfectly blue. Now I look exactly like the others in all the places where my body is covered with fabric.

Present colors! This command, issued to the honor guard by a girl standing in front of the assembly, calls our eyes to order. Now all of us are required to gaze at the three pupils who are bringing us the flag, the one marching in front is the flag-bearer, he holds the pole to which the flag is affixed, and the two others walking behind him form the honor guard's train, the flag itself has no train and hangs straight down because no wind is blowing. All eyes are fixed on the trio with the flag, we stand in the schoolyard in a square, only one edge of this square has been left open, the one facing the entrance to the school, and it is to the center of this open edge that the honor guard is marching, the rest of us stand along the other three sides of the square with the smallest in front and the taller ones in back, each row of toes lining up perfectly, right hands held to caps in a salute, and from this moment on I can no longer allow my gaze to wander across the blue and white water above which the other children's heads are bobbing like flesh-colored buoys, heads that cannot be made identical to one another without masks, no more than can the naked bits of knee sticking out between stockings and skirts, knees that are crooked, fat or pointy, scraped or dimpled, but definitely tan in this land of eternal summer. I gaze at the flag and wonder whether the teachers who have stipulated where our eyes must rest can see our gazes crisscrossing through the air, aimed at the trio with the flag like so many lances.

One. Two. And three. During the first three years of school, we are required to cross our arms if we wish to rest them on our desktops when we aren't writing. Only when we are older, the teachers say, will we be permitted to lay one arm smooth and straight atop the other. When we pray, each hand rests flat against the other, no interlocking of fingers allowed. When it's time for recess, we exit the classroom one behind the other in single file, nice and slow, the teachers say. One. Two. And three. All rapid motions, everything that is sudden or askew, all running, swinging, shoving, lolling and falling, all spinning in circles and jumping, has been cut off from us, brought to a place where it is inaccessible to us and left for scrap. Just like bicycles no longer fit for use, all these things twist together in a heap, intertwining to form a mass that can never again be disentangled, and in the end all of it decomposes collectively, as if it had always been of a piece. One.

During recess we crouch in the shade of the big tree—no shouting, children, no fighting—gathering up the firebugs that live at the base of its trunk, filling our hands with them, or else with gravel and grains of sand, and when an airplane flies past overhead, one of us whispers louder than the other: My parents are up there, they're on their way to Alaska, or: That's my mother's airplane, she's traveling to Rome, or: Today my father's sitting in that plane up there, he's flying far far away, where's he going, really far away, well if you don't even know where he's going then it can't be true, yes it is, my father's even flying across the ocean, well so where's he going. Really far away. That's stupid. No shouting. We're winning, my friend Anna whispers to us, we're winning, she always says that when a tire blows out somewhere outside, the noise it makes sounds like gunfire, sometimes there are many shots in a row. We're winning, she whispers, and then all of us fall silent, waiting to see if we really are winning.

This time we didn't win, my friend Anna says a day later. My mother, she says, climbed over the fence to give the horses something to eat. And one of the horses wasn't really tame yet, it shied away from her and didn't want to eat anything. And when she got closer, it reared up on its hind legs. And then, I ask. Then it came down on its hooves and almost hit my mother in the head, so she tried to run away. But she didn't manage to get back over the fence in time, and then the horse saw she was scared of it and came after her. And if she hadn't been afraid? Then the horse would have remained calm. But it saw she was afraid. And then it came after her and kicked her and threw itself on top of her with all its weight. But horses never kick people, I say. Not if they're tame, Anna says, but this horse was basically still wild. Oh, I say. And then the other horses got carried away as well. They remembered how they used to be wild. And then? Then all the horses ran over my mother. With their hooves. My mother was an Indian, Anna says to me. I don't say anything. She climbed over the fence to feed her horses, she says, and then her very own horses trampled her to death. Just imagine, Anna says to me. I imagine this, and then say to my friend: I think that's a good way for an Indian to die. I think so too, Anna says. Were you there? I ask. No, Anna says. And the horses? They had to shoot them, of course. You heard the shots yourself. Yes, I say, that's true.

A music box is playing: *Plume in the summer wind, waywardly swaying, thus heart of womankind everyway bendeth*. The music box is on a table with wheels that my mother and father roll into my room in the morning. Flowers and candlelight, and beside the music box are the presents. It's my birthday. One day out of all the days of the year is the day when I was born. One day out of all the days of the year is the first day. Or is it better just to dive into the wet concrete right away and let the first day be the last. Open your eyes, behold the grave and then dive right in and turn to stone. *Plume in the summer wind*. I am given a silver barrette, a book of faerie tales, letter paper with a watermark and my name in the upper left-hand corner, a soup dish on the bottom of which two girls are playing ball, and a Rose of Jericho, a dried-up thing that becomes a flower when you wet it. Until the dish breaks, the girls will go on playing ball at the bottom of the porcelain. Until water is in sight, the

Rose of Jericho will keep rolling through the desert. The dish will not break. When I have spooned up enough soup that the girls begin to play beneath the noodles and greens, I put my ear to the dish to listen, I want to hear one or the other of them catching the ball. My mother says there's nothing to hear because the ball is suspended in midair between them. And it will never come down? No, my mother says, it's a picture. We are so happy you were born. A picture always remains just as it is.

Saint Difunta Correa died of thirst in the desert, but the child drinking at her breast was still alive when the two of them were found. Drinking life from a dead woman, my wet-nurse smoothes the little picture with her index finger, it's odd, when the life leaves a body, this makes it heavier rather than lighter. The saint's back, legs and heels press heavily into the sand as she holds the child in her arms, yes, holds it, the dead woman is still holding a living child in her arms, which are already dead, and the third figure in this alliance is the silent sun beating down upon the two of them, the sun that caused the death of the mother. Wherever there is an altar in the sand for this saint who died of thirst, travelers leave bottles of water as offerings, my wet-nurse says. I wonder whether the water can summon her back to life. Whether a saint who has been dead so long can drink her life back out of all these many sealed bottles. Does a saint even have hands and a mouth. My wet nurse says she will most assuredly get up again. Yes, but when. When no one comes any longer to leave new offerings, she says. When silence reigns on earth, she won't be able to resist looking to see what's going on, then at the latest she will get up again and drink.

So the story does go on. To the right and left and above and below the edges of the picture. Of course, my wet nurse says. And only as far as the picture extends do things remain as they are. That's right, she says and lets me hold the little card with the image of the Difunta. But all around the picture things remain in motion, I ask, even this story itself which cannot go any farther here in the picture. Most certainly, my wet nurse says. You can see, she says, how for example the sun is moving across the sky. Yes, I say, that's true, that's how you can tell. It would be awful, she says, if the sun were always as high up in the sky as here above the two people in the picture. It would burn everything up. That's true, I say, looking at the bars of light on the floor of my room put there by the sun slipping between the blinds. My wet nurse takes back the picture of the saint and puts it in her olive colored bag. Outside it's noon.

I wonder if the sun can wear out. In countries like this, where it must shine day after day all year round, does it get shabby more quickly than elsewhere. In countries like this, where it can see everything at almost every moment except during the night or when, as rarely happens, it is raining, is the sun marked by what it sees. Are the things taking place beneath its rays reflected back at it. So that the sun itself, depending what it illuminates, appears perfect or rumpled, healthy or cold. Is this what sometimes makes it turn white. Or blotchy. All that looking. Probably. While I kneel and get up again and sit down again and then kneel again, performing the roundelay of prayer Sunday after Sunday in the crepuscular church, I am thinking of the Holy Trinity: mother, infant and sun.

Hot, my mother says, pulling me away from the stove. Hot, my father says whenever anyone's making a fire, and he positions himself between me and the fire. Hot, my mother says as she lights the candle to place inside my St. Martin's Day lantern. *Star light star bright, first star I see tonight*. When the candle's little shade has been drawn all around it like an accordion, I am permitted to take the lantern by its long wooden stick and go outside with it. *I wish I may, I wish I might*. The shade is made of paper. Am I made of paper too, I ask my mother. My mother laughs and says: Of course not, and calls out to my father that I just asked if I was made of paper, and my father laughs too, comes out of his room into the hallway and fondles my head. Then I go out onto the street with my mother and see children coming out of all the other houses with lanterns in their hands, on St. Martin's we're all allowed to stay up past midnight and brighten the dark streets with our lanterns. If I were made of paper, first my dress would catch fire, then my legs, then my arms, then my head, basically all the parts farthest from the center, and only then would my stomach start to burn, and the little pink buttons above my heart, and finally the heart itself, the most interior part of me. All these things would turn black and keep flying up into the night as long as they continued to smolder, and only after the air had cooled them down would they return to earth in a rain of ashes. But I am not made of paper, my mother repeats. Nonetheless she pulls me away any time I want to touch fire, saying: Hot.

Eyes, nose, mouth. How often my mother shut her eyes the instant before my index finger hit its mark, how often my father opened his mouth to show me what a mouth is and then closed it around my finger as if he were going to bite, but he didn't bite. If you wanted to play ball with someone's head, only one thing would get in the way: the nose. My father's teeth are very white, and when I probe around inside his dark mouth with my finger, they feel damp and hard. I see a tree and say tree, I smell the cake my mother bakes on Sunday and say cake, I hear a bird twittering in the garden, and my mother says: That's right, a bird. We put the cake into our mouths, it vanishes there, mouth, eyes and nose: holes, the beginnings of paths, no one knows quite where they lead. Stomach, my mother says, I've never seen my stomach from the inside, but at least what I eat comes out again on the other end, but what about the things I put into my eyes, where do they go, are all of them supposed to fit inside my head, even if I were to stack them up the way our housekeeper stacks the laundry, folding it and placing one piece atop the other, there still wouldn't be room, I don't think, and therefore I keep saying all the things I'm seeing so they'll change course inside my head and go out again through my mouth. Shit, I say later when I see what has become of the cake. That's a filthy word, my mother says, wiping my bottom. Don't say words like that, she says and flushes. But it's something we ate. That was before, my mother says, and we go back to the other room. So the cake has gotten dirty on its way through my body. You can't look at it that way, my father says, it doesn't have anything to do with you, it's just a matter of the word. I'm not allowed to say it. No, my mother says, words like that should never cross the lips of a young lady. Eyes. Nose. Mouth. So it's precisely the things that are filthy that are supposed to be stacked up and stored in my head and aren't allowed to change course and go out again through my mouth. But, I say, if I see a foot that is dirty and say foot, then that's a filthy word too, isn't it, but my mother says no, the word itself is clean. Aha. It's only the word shit I'm not supposed to say, but now that's really quite enough, my mother says. My father says: time for a walk. The obelisk stands at the eye of the city, on the large square with cars circling around it, since yesterday it's been wearing a wooden skirt; I slide my hand across the white letters on the fence boards, there's a spotlight shining on them, and my father reads aloud: Silence is health.

Maintaining an equilibrium, my father said one day when I came home from school with my hair disheveled, by no means depends on the physical strength possessed by you or your opponent, equilibrium is always an equilibrium of the means you employ. On this occasion my father showed me a maneuver that lets you twist an attacking arm onto your opponent's back before he even knows what's happening and in this way hold and overpower him. Whenever I played shop as a little girl, I always gave my customers play money along with the marbles I was selling instead of requesting payment. I hadn't yet understood that even in buying and selling there is an invisible equilibrium to be upheld, one utterly indifferent to the often shabby appearance of the coins. If all the maneuvers my father has employed while rubbing the holster of his service weapon until it is shiny have served to preserve some equilibrium or other, then this light, invisible weapon assuredly balances out many things whose nature is not immediately apparent to me upon gazing only at his gun or its holster.

But this time we won, my friend Anna says to me in the schoolyard, nudging the ball this way and that with her feet. No one in the whole world plays better than we do. We're the champions. Anna's soccer ball hits a pebble and changes course. Two to one, she says, now it's been proven. She runs after the ball. And that's why they're setting off fireworks now, she shouts, coming to a halt beside the ball, we can hear the explosions, but because the brick wall all around our schoolyard is so high and perhaps also because, as always, the sun is shining, we can see neither flowers nor rings of fire nor shooting stars nor golden rain in the sky. Maybe they forgot about the sun, Anna says, stepping back at an angle for a running start, then she kicks the ball, shooting it at me, that is, at the goal behind me, which I am guarding, I'm the goalie, and the goal is a bit of grass between an empty milk carton on the right and a stone wastepaper basket on the left, I step to one side of the goal I am guarding, and the ball hurtles into it. If it had struck me, I'd be dead. That isn't fair, Anna says. Plenty of room on a soccer field like this, and as for the grass, the softer the better. Body after body beneath the grass, hands outspread, and above all these hands, mouths and eyes, the ball rolls toward the goal and gently glides into it, we're the champions.

I am sleeping. My grandmother is telling my aunt how she got dizzy that morning. A free-of-charge carousel ride, she says, all the cupboards were dancing around me in a circle, I was seeing stars, and then everything went black. Then I heard the angels singing, my grandmother says. Free of charge. She laughs. My mother says to her brother, my uncle: All the same, I think it's funny she hasn't called. After all, she's our sister. I even told her she could stay with us. And my aunt laughs too and says, oh, you don't even have to be so old to fall, our neighbor fell off the roof of his shed last Sunday, he wanted to look over the edge to see if he'd left his hammer down there, so he bent over, but then his rear end wanted to look too and came sliding down on top of him, and the next thing he knew he was lying on the ground. The neighbor. Well, maybe he'd also had a bit too much to drink, my grandmother says. Quite possible, my aunt says. My uncle says, you've got to remember what she must be going through with such a husband. Well, then let her bring him too, my mother says. My uncle doesn't say anything. None of this makes any sense to me, my mother says. My uncle says to my father, two to one, not bad, eh? And my father replies, we're the champions now. My uncle says, I never thought I'd see the day, and laughs, and my father laughs too, and my aunt says, well, it's true a person shouldn't start drinking in the morning, and my grandmother gives no response. I am lying on the floor, asleep. My mother says, how can she sleep like that, on the floor in the middle of the room, and everyone looks at me for a moment, no one says anything, then my mother says, let me go see if dinner's ready. My aunt says, but you definitely shouldn't wash the windows by yourself any more, that ladder really is dangerous. My mother calls out: Dinner's ready. *Be present at our table, Lord, be here and everywhere adored. Your mercies bless, and grant that we may feast in Paradise with Thee.*

The table we sit down at is large and oval, like a stadium. Uncle and aunt, mother and father, father at the narrow curve at the end of the table, grandmother beside me. There's fish for dinner. The young woman at the far end of the table, directly opposite my father, declines without a word when the housekeeper wants to put some on her plate. The young man sitting to my left also helps himself only to vegetables. The housekeeper plucks a thread from his shirt before she goes on serving, and my mother says: The flies are such a nuisance this year. The housekeeper smiles at me. The two strangers slowly manipulate their knives and forks, silently chewing. I point at them with my knife, asking who these people are who are eating with us, but before my question can slip out between fish and bones, my grandmother says, don't wave your knife around in the air, and my mother says, don't talk when you're eating fish.

Snow. Knives and forks clinking against porcelain, jawbones hinging open with a faint cracking sound, my father pulverizes the fish-bones between his teeth instead of drawing them out of his mouth one by one, the sparkling water sings in its goblets. If snow were to start falling now, falling on the table-cloth, on the hair of my mother and father, on hands and into goblets, then eventually you wouldn't hear any of this any longer. In the beginning, the snow will melt because the things it is falling on are still warm, that's what my grandmother told me, but sooner or later the cold starts to get the better of the warmth, she said, that's always how it goes if it keeps snowing long enough, the snow covers everything up and then all is still. If it were to start snowing now, the entire family would fall silent all at once. White, soft and as motion-less as the fish we are eating. My grandmother is the only one in our family who can still remember snow.

When my grandmother was a young girl, she once laced her legs so tightly into ice skates that to this day you can see purple marks under her knees. Snow is edible, she said. She sewed a little cap for my mother during that one cold winter she spent with her in the old country, a cap that could be tied beneath the chin, with a wooly ball on top. So my mother too was once an infant—but far from here, long ago, on the other side of the world, wrapped up in blankets, lying on a sled with frozen-red cheeks—which in this black-and-white photograph are distinctly gray. On the other side of the world. The surface of the photo has cracks in it because of the long journey on which my grandmother carried it with her. But to this day the cap remains undamaged, it lies in a stack of carnival costumes in a heavy leather suitcase in the storeroom. My mother's eyes are the color of water, they look like melted snow. My eyes are black. I don't know what snow is, and there was never a time when I did know this. On this side of the world.

When fish is served, everyone is given a special knife that isn't sharp. But when we are eating meat, I have to use my child's knife, the handle of which has a cat's face engraved in it. Then my mother cuts my meat into little pieces with her knife, which is pointed and jagged-edged, and my knife with the cat is only for pushing the bits she's cut onto my fork. The handle of my fork has a bear on it, and the spoon has a rabbit. If a knife is sharp enough, you can cut all the way around the soles of a man's or even a woman's feet and then peel back the skin. After all, this man or this woman will no longer have far to walk to reach the land of the dead. And some word is always the last one. Knife perhaps. Or some other one. Some word this man or this woman has always known.

No one knows for sure anymore, my wet-nurse says to me, whether the Difunta had already given birth to her child before she set out on her journey or whether the child was born in the desert. Why did she take a trip in the first place, I ask. The child's father was imprisoned one hundred and fifty kilometers away, she replies. Behind bars on the other side of the desert. She was on her way to see him, my wet-nurse says.

Did you know, Marie says, that where our garden is there used to be desert. Marie is scooping sand into a small metal pail with her hands. I have never seen the garden belonging to my wet-nurse and her daughter Marie, who is something like my milk-sister. A long time before I was born, Marie says, my mother stuck a few scrawny little trees into the desert and hoped for rain. And did it rain, I ask. Uh-huh, says Marie, whose bucket is nearly full already. Next to the bucket I have been digging a hole with a shovel and finally have reached the depth at which the sand becomes firmer and shimmers dark and moist at the edges of the pit. The shadows the trees cast on the sand are no thicker than threads of tar, but in these threads the rain has gotten caught. Now I can finally empty the sugar sand from Marie's bucket into my hole. Later everything grew. Flowers. Even grass. That's right, Marie says and gets up so as to take me by one hand and one foot and spin me around in a circle so fast that my own weight carries me out of this orbit into the sand. I land right in a thicket of unfamiliar arms and legs.

My wet-nurse is sitting in the shade beneath an umbrella, her skin very white against the brown pattern of her bathing suit. This section of beach is reserved for women and children, and beside it is the section for men. Swimming lovers tryst along the rope that cuts the sea in two, touching beneath the water's surface. In places where warm and cold water are not clearly separated, my father told me not long ago, currents are produced, the intersection of the warm and the cold sets the water in motion. My father knows all about currents. From time to time, little groups of women rise to their feet on the beach and start clapping their hands, one of them holding on her shoulder the child that has lost track of its mother, nanny or aunt and now is crying. Mother, nanny or aunt hears the clapping and comes running up to claim her child. Gray-haired old women are playing cards, the heads of women are lying there, eyes closed, and feet running down to the water thrust their toes into the sand between the cheeks of these women, children are building sandcastles and moats that fill up and empty again with each wave. There is plenty of empty space between the men on the other side, but here where the women and children are, each lying, sitting or standing body is packed in among many others.

When I get home from the beach, sand between my toes, my hair matted from the salt water, I find the young woman who ate with us not long ago sitting in my room on the sofa, reading a book. Her clothes are covered with dust. I was just passing the time until you came back, she says, and lays the book aside. Could I have something to drink. I say: One moment, and go down to the kitchen. I open the icebox and

gaze into it for a while: sausage, cheese, yogurt. I gaze into it.
Fruit, vegetables, ketchup and eggs. I shiver. A pot filled with
yesterday's leftovers. I gaze into the cool, illuminated window,
and everything I might be capable of thinking freezes solid.
There is a half-full bottle of mineral water in the icebox door,
I grab it and a glass and bring both of them to where my
visitor is waiting. Do you know how to swim, the woman asks
me after she has filled the glass with water and emptied it at a
single draught. Yes, I say. When I was your age, she says, I
used to dive for combs. In the ocean, I ask. No, in the swimming pool, of course, she says, smiling. The sea, she says,
carries off everything you throw in it, quicker than you can
imagine. My father knows all about currents, I say. I see, the
woman says.

She's got a fever, my father says, laying his heavy hand on my
forehead. I am lying there trying to decipher the pattern
printed on the wallpaper, but I can't make sense of it: moons,
archways, something or other whose corners ought to overlap
but have been left open, I can't make sense of what I'm
looking at. I shut my eyes. She'll feel better once she's slept,
my mother says. The light in my room is dim because the
blinds have been lowered, but if the window were open, I
could raise my eyelids and see the burning mountains from my

bed, could peer through my window as if through a magnifying glass at the huge, red and blue shimmering rock formation, this motionless beast on the horizon whose thirst has gone unslaked for centuries, not even moss can grow on it. Or have my eyelids themselves become heavy curtains blocking my view of this fire that has turned to stone. Oh, not at all. Just try taking a stroll all the way across the city and then through the city's outskirts, which used to be desert, and then through the desert itself all the way to the mountains. Or else it's nighttime. She's burning up, my mother says. The mountains don't burn at night. Watch out, it's hot. Only between two and seven. When the sun's on its way downhill. I could gaze at a chair, a table, a door. But the mountains are too much for my gaze to hold, they are bellowing and bursting my eyeballs. Do you think she's in pain, my mother asks my father. Now the animal is rending my hair with its stone teeth, tearing out huge chunks of it, even your own mother won't recognize you, eye sockets empty, the skull hairless, nice and cool, at last I am seeing the fire creature up close. I don't think so, my father says. In my blindness I can finally see that this creature intends to drink me dry. Would you call the doctor, my mother says to my father. She places a cool cloth on my lips. How long do you think the Difunta Correa lay in the desert before they found her. I don't know, my wet-nurse says.

Hours. Or days. At night it gets cold in the desert. Yes, she says. Pink room for a girl. Home. At home.

Well, young lady, says my father's friend, the doctor who is standing beside my bed when I wake up. Now we're going to cook the goose of that fever of yours. Open your mouth, he says and shoves a spoon containing a bitter liquid into it. *Bumped his head as he went to bed*, I can hear somebody singing. The doctor is a tall man with a hairless skull. His mouth keeps smiling as he pours his medicine into me, but with his eyes he's watching to make sure the medicine disappears completely inside me. *It's raining, it's pouring*—and then comes the snow. My grandmother is the only one in the family who can still remember snow. He puts one hand on my forehead, nods in my mother's direction and says, she'll be fine again in no time. My mother says she's sometimes heard me talking to myself even without a fever. What was his opinion of that? It's a stage children go through, says my father's friend, the doctor, girls especially. And he snaps shut his bag in which he keeps his implements and medications. *Couldn't get up in the morning.* My mother says to me: You'll see, any minute now those nasty bacteria will give up the ghost. The doctor says: They're already thrashing about and gasping for breath. My mother says: And they're screaming for help, but no one's going to help them, you'll see. But, I say. I can hear the singing inside me. No buts, the doctor says, you'll be fit as a fiddle in no time.

I am lying in bed, and in my body the goose of my illness is being cooked, what goose is that, our housekeeper is vacuuming, and when it's quiet I know she's still there all the same, she's polishing the mirrors, cleaning my piano down in the living room, scrubbing a sink or a tub, putting clean sheets on my parents' bed, ironing. Or else. She's gone out after all, to do the shopping, pick fruit in the garden. My forehead is cooler than during the night, I have burrowed deep into my pillow and lie there, eyes open, gazing at the garlands of roses printed on the wallpaper in my room, I can recognize the roses as roses again, I am trying to distinguish the silence of being alone from the other silence. Around noon I hear noises down below, the housekeeper is setting to work in the kitchen, stirring, blending and chopping, icebox open, icebox shut, she is making lunch for my mother and me. I don't feel like eating. The goose. In the afternoon there are dishes to wash, far in the distance I hear plates clacking together, the sound muted by water and suds, and in the silence that follows I know the washing machine is being filled with dirty laundry, shortly afterward its drum begins to revolve, I can't keep my eyes open, an hour or two later the machine wakes me, wailing and vibrating in its spin cycle, then everything is silent once more, the housekeeper carries the laundry out into the garden and hangs it on the clothesline in the fresh air.

Ever since our housekeeper's husband went away and her son, as she says, struck out on his own, she's been sharing an apart-ment with her father-in-law. The two of them were left behind. So to speak. As the housekeeper says. The house-keeper says: My father-in-law can't walk so well anymore. He needs a cane. Or she says: I definitely want to see this movie with my father-in-law. Or: My father-in-law doesn't like pota-toes. When she says anything at all. Sometimes she smiles when our paths cross in the house. When I ask my mother where her husband is, my mother says: One doesn't ask such things, it's none of our business. She could marry her father-in-law, I say. It's none of our business, my mother says. By the time you get married, everything will be all right again, my father said to me, standing beside my sickbed. How old is she, I ask. About my age, my mother says, and then she says: No more questions. Oh, I say, I thought she was an old woman already. I don't want to hear another word about it, my mother says, and points to my math textbook with her pen. I look at my math book and don't say anything else, but I am thinking that our housekeeper looks much older than my mother, she looks old enough to be my grandmother, and her bones are very brittle too. All she has to do is stumble to break her foot, and when she knocks on a door too energetically, her wrist-bone splinters. She says it's called bones of glass when a person has bones like that, and since parts of her are always shattering, she's often out sick, and then my mother has to do all the cooking, ironing and cleaning herself. A squared plus B squared equals C squared. I try to imagine how transparent our housekeeper is on the inside with all her glass bones. If she never remarries, when will everything be all right again. Will things just go on like that until she's broken into a thousand tiny particles and has to be swept up with a dustpan and brush, on and on until everything will never be all right again.

That the child survived has to be a miracle, I say to my wet-nurse. We're on our way to the market-hall, she's letting me carry the basket. Besides us there isn't anyone at all on the street. Of course it is, my wet-nurse says. The side of the street we are walking on lies in the shade of the buildings. If the mother had survived, too, it wouldn't have been a miracle. No, my wet-nurse says, probably not. Then it would just have been a difficult journey. Probably, my wet-nurse says. We have the sidewalk all to ourselves, block after block. They would simply have gotten where they were going eventually. Yes, my wet-nurse says. So it's only because the mother died that there was room for a miracle. You can't look at it like that, my wet-nurse says to me. We turn the corner to the left and find ourselves in bright sunshine. The air's so hot it's turned to liquid. An old woman comes holding dozens upon dozens of empty plastic bags, white, pink and orange, that are puffing up in a breeze I cannot feel and rustling, the entire woman is puffed up and rustles as she walks, I half expect her to flap these inferior wings and sail into the air before she reaches us. But she just brushes past us with all that emptiness clutched in her hands and laughs in my direction, she even looks back at me over her shoulder to give me the chance to gaze at her longer. And Jesus is dead too, I say. Of course, my wet-nurse says. A few meters more, then we step sideways out of the heat into the gossipy shadows of the hall, which is crammed with people.

It's perfectly fine with me, the teacher says, if you have lots of lights on in the room you're in. But please turn off all the lights you aren't using. We nod. My lower arms are lying neatly one atop the other. Save electricity, the teacher says. Think of our country. Just look at yourselves, the teacher says, you have on clean clothes, you go to school, you have enough to eat. But these things don't come about automatically, the teacher says. This here is just a beginning, he says, imagine there were only water all around us. My father knows all about currents. If all of us work together, we can create new land using the sand that washes up, the teacher says. And all the people who will live on this new land will be just as well off as you. We nod. But the sea is treacherous, he says, and what we manage to wrest from it here might well be taken away from us someplace else. Have you ever seen the sea crashing against the cliffs? We nod. An island needs cliffs to keep the sea from sweeping it into the sea. Cliffs day in and day out. And do you know what it looks like beneath the sea. We shake our heads. Do you know what monsters live at a depth of four thousand meters? We shake our heads. It isn't possible to know them, the teacher says.

Do you hear that, Anna says to me during recess when a shot rings out behind the red brick wall surrounding our schoolyard: That was my sister. We can't see anything. We wait for what will happen next. Now it's his turn, Anna says. Whose turn, I ask. The one who's in love with her. But only if he has the courage. A second shot rings out. We won, Anna shouts. Who won, I ask. He and my sister. Did they rob a bank? No, she says, it's something completely different. What sort of thing, I ask. Love, she says. If everything went well, both of them are dead now.

The Mazurka in F minor is the last piece Chopin wrote. They found it on his deathbed, my piano teacher says. My piano teacher always draws the curtains when she's giving a lesson so that of the sunshine outside the window all that makes its way into the room is a sulfurous light, this sulfurous light comes to rest on the piano keys, making them look like the worn-out teeth of someone who's smoked too much all his life. Besides the piano, the room contains a few chairs scattered about and a desk whose top is scratched. Some of the desk drawers are ajar, you can see there's nothing in them except for one which has an empty, wadded-up milk carton stuffed inside; the room smells of the milk's sour dregs. Milk. Drink. The place where I go for piano lessons is a public music school. The floors are linoleum-covered, the walls lined with soundproof insulation. The wastepaper basket is overflowing, and between the windows hangs a photograph of snow-capped mountains. My grandmother is the only one in the family who can still remember snow. Everything in the room —desk, chairs and piano—is somehow off-kilter. All the rooms in the school are like this, my lessons take place now in one room, now in another, one-hundred-seventeen, one-hundred-fifteen, three-twenty-eight, two-hundred-eleven, there are three entire floors of these rooms branching off the long corridors, and if it isn't mountains covered in snow, it's a big lake so big that nothing is reflected in it, and if it isn't a milk carton, it's a ball of crumpled-up music paper, and if the soundproof insulation has a hole in one spot, you can hear how, in the next room. How in the next room. How in the next room someone is playing the Mazurka in F minor, Chopin's last composition, which they found on his death-bed.

Indistinguishable rooms, each just the same as every other one, *how sour sweet music is*, at the auditions for this school a girl with red hair sang a song I didn't know, we were free to choose, to sing anything we felt like, and the song this girl felt like singing resulted in her being expelled from the room. I'd picked the song of our homeland, my and my father's song. This school is a gift, the woman overseeing the auditions had said as she was signing my acceptance form, a gift from whom, I'd wanted to ask but didn't get a chance to, a few students here, the woman went on to say, are ungrateful and fail to understand that a person is responsible for gifts he is given. But it is also true, I wanted to say later, when I was already familiar with the lopsided furniture and the yellow wool curtains and the smell of sour milk: No one is at home here, and at night the school is all alone. If you ever see anyone damage school property or leave trash behind, the woman had said to us, come tell me. But no one going into a room in this school ever sees another person, I thought to myself later, and the only time you hear anything of the other pupils is when the soundproof insulation has a hole in one spot, there's never anyone in sight, the corridors are always empty, and all the rooms look just the same. The trash is always there already, along with the lopsidedness and scratches. Maybe there aren't even any other pupils besides me. I'm supposed to tidy up the school one room at a time. It's certainly possible. Only a person who appreciates beauty can make music, the woman said that day as we sat around her in a circle. I never again saw anyone from this circle at the school. But my teacher doesn't say a word about this. In any case, it wasn't me who wadded up the milk carton and stuck it in the drawer, I say to her, and she replies: I know. Even my teacher is always just sitting in a chair beside the piano when I come in, she is waiting for me, and as she waits she leafs through her sheet music, the part in her hair is reflected in the gleaming black of the piano. My piano lesson is never cancelled, and the teacher is always there before me, she is always already sitting there, waiting. She, too, pays no attention to anything that might, behind her back, be standing open, scratched or starting to smell rancid. And even when I shut the double door behind me, she doesn't get up. She just nods in my direction and smiles, and her prominent cheekbones turn her eyes into slits, I shut the double door behind me, she says Hello and shakes hands with me when I have reached our instrument, without getting to her feet. So it must be better, I think, just to leave everything the way it is. Let the school spend the night all alone. Let anyone who wants to go around at night spilling milk. I play. Press the keys down as deep as you can, my teacher says, and go even deeper once the note has sounded, it makes a difference. Keep your little finger on its tip, and change the pedal cleanly. Staccato. Count to yourself. When the same note is to be struck more than once, change fingers, but make each attack exactly as strong as the one before. There's a different photograph of our country hanging in every room, the woman overseeing the auditions had told us that day, but I have never seen mountains capped with snow, neither from my window nor on any trip. Our country is larger than you can imagine, the woman says, some day you too will see snow.

When my mother picks me up from piano lessons, I go hopping beside her from island to island across the city's stone carpet patterns: on black, white or gray. Those who. Then their friends. The ones who remember. Who are afraid. And finally everyone. Why can't I ever go home all by myself, I ask my mother. Because you're still too little for that, she says and takes my hand to cross the street. First look to the left to see if a car is coming, she says, and then to the right, and if nothing's coming, hurry across.

What's your name, where do you live. When I open the door to my room, it scrapes the wood in one spot, the floor in that spot has been marked in a semicircle by the opening door, but out in the hallway the floor is made of stone, stone that was once sand at the bottom of the sea, you can still see curved and spiral-shaped shells in it, but now it's hard and the shells are fixed in place and flat, the stone has been cut into slices slab after slab, there's a sweetish smell in the bathroom, the smell of powder, my father and mother put a little in their shoes before they go out, if you turn the faucet too far to the left, the water comes out of the pipes boiling hot, be careful not to burn yourself, my father says, take the hair out of the comb after you comb your hair, my mother says, when you hold the toilet paper up to the light, it looks almost like milk glass, I wash my feet in the bidet, what's your name, where do you live. So-and-so. One-A, Such-and-such Street. When I go down the curved staircase, I always keep to the outer edge, the steps there are so wide there's room for my whole foot, close to the center I might slip, my mother explained and said: Be careful, and took me by the hand when I was still little, and when I want to unlock the lower part of the sideboard, I have to turn the key once to the right, but when I want to lock it, twice to the left, I'll never understand that, in front of the fireplace is a little brick platform covered with turquoise tiles, if I want I can set up shop there and sell paper fruit, or else lay my doll there. So-and-so. One-A, Such-and-such Street. Who used to live in this house, I ask my father. A person who got up to crooked business involving money, my father says. And the house was full of cats. House. Home. At home.

I see a long hallway with a room at the end that is my room. A bed and chest of drawers, and high up on the right is the window. Dreaming of a witch with an axe in her hand, I clamber over the fence to join Hansel and Gretel, but then fall out of bed. Backwards. Back to the endless hallway stretching on and on into the distance, now there's a woman sitting on the floor, upon her knees a rug that's been cut into strips, she is sewing them together end to end. To cover the hallway floor, she says. The bumpy wooden floor that vanishes in the shadows before the door to my room. Further back. To the left, my parents' room. My parents are nowhere to be seen.

The door is standing open. Inside, a black leather sofa with a visitor seated on it, a woman I don't know. Further. On the wall to the right, the kitchen light switch. A figure sits atop the switch, encircling it with its wire legs, a skinny man with glasses. I can't yet reach the switch. In the kitchen, a table, and on the table, a dirty teaspoon lying facedown. A banquette surrounds the kitchen table. I flip up its lid and see shoes. I knock into the table, the spoon falls to the floor with a clatter. Out of the room, moving backward. Further back. A mop leaning against the wall. The washrag hanging from it is still damp. And finally one last room just beside the front door, to the right or left I couldn't say, a room that's all lit up, someone sits there writing. Then my back thumps against the door, the big white door through which you enter.

And then comes the evening when I am left alone, I want to go to the neighbors' but can't find my way, in the stairwell I am suddenly standing at the foot of a ramp made of concrete that doesn't lead anywhere. I stand there waiting. Was that a dream, I ask my parents. Of course they say, or do you imagine we would ever leave you all by yourself? And what sort of concrete is that supposed to have been, my mother asks, not to mention: What stairwell. I'm not sure, I say, but it was definitely a ramp made of concrete, I was standing at the bottom and it was nighttime. And what neighbors. I don't know, I say. But in the stairwell it smelled of fish. When did you dream all this? my father asks. A long time ago, I say. There, you see, he replies, when you're a child, you can't yet tell the difference between dreams and reality. He takes me in his arms, my mother laughs and goes into the kitchen. My parents have plenty of room. But I don't, not really. The head I inhabit was already furnished with other people's dreams for as long as I can remember, it seems to me. So then I fall down from time to time, or else I run into something, or get stuck. Father and mother.

You play beautifully, says the young woman leaning against my piano. The young man is sitting in the armchair beside her, one leg crossed over the other, waving his feet in time to the music as I play. He is staring off into space and appears to be waiting in no hurry at all for something that's about to happen. I used to like to sing, the young woman says. What I liked about it was that you can express anything you want without there being anything to see. Or touch. It's always only the air moving. You can even sing, she says, without there being anything to hear. You can sing on the inside. Do you know what I mean? Yes, I say. Do you like to go to piano lessons, the young woman asks. Yes, I say. Time for dinner, my mother calls from downstairs. I have to go, I say, nod to the two people and leave the room. When I open the door, it scrapes the wooden floor in a semicircle. Out in the hallway the floor is made of stone.

We wanted our daughter to learn an instrument, my father says to his friend. The friend has a pointy white beard which holds his face like a bowl made of hair, the bowl nods, making the face nod along with it, and the man says: Yes, that's good, and sticks a new bite of food in his mouth that he speared on his fork as my father was talking about me. She's taking piano lessons, my father says. My father doesn't say: Our daughter is learning how to set the air in motion. An instrument. I press a key, and the air starts moving. In the piano case standing upright before me, my teacher's eyes are reflected, and my own as well. I have no idea what's going on inside. Inside the case, the pressure of my hands is being transformed into the Mazurka in F minor, the piece that was found on Chopin's deathbed. The fork is no doubt an instrument as well. While the man, my father's friend, is now chewing, his beard moves up and down. Was Chopin just lying there with his mouth and eyes open, still holding the music paper in his waxy hands? Probably, my teacher says. Head scrapes paper, paper cuts finger, finger twirls the air, air, head, music. After dinner the man with the beard lays his napkin to one side and gets up from the table to smoke a cigar with my father in his room. The meat has been transformed within him, inside his body, into getting up and walking, I can't see from the outside exactly how, his shirt doesn't even show me my reflection, it has a checked pattern. A person has to eat, my aunt says. Meat, vegetables and bread are transformed into walking, coughing and laughing, into skin, eyes, fingernails and hair, the body itself is an instrument playing itself. You have to eat if you want to set yourself in motion, you don't have a choice. And drink as well, if you want to keep your mind clear, my aunt says. Through the closed door comes the smell of tobacco. Yes, drinking is important, she says to my grandmother. And when my grandmother isn't there, she says to my mother: It's happened before that she was disoriented because she hadn't drunk enough. Our daughter is learning to play an instrument, my father says. The music itself I cannot grasp.

A tiny house. It doesn't even reach to my knees. It's open in the front, you can look right into the ground floor and the attic. On the ground floor, three Difunta Correas made of plaster are lying in a row, each with a plaster child at her breast. The paint that has made their clothes red or blue is already flaking. In the attic several jam jars hold flowers. And where the saint's garden ought to be, in front of the house, a few bottles have been stuck in the earth, filled or half-filled with water and screwed tightly shut. The house doesn't have to be any bigger because the Difuntas are never getting up again. And their children won't grow either, at least not on this altar. I ask my wet-nurse: Do you think in real life the child is now old and gray? Maybe, my wet-nurse says. Or maybe has grandchildren already? Maybe, my wet-nurse says. The tiny altar before which we are standing was built next to a bus stop in the dusty grass. My wet-nurse discovered it on her way home, she wanted me to see it, as this was an example of a place, she said, where the saint and her child are finally in the shade.

At a bus stop on the way home, a woman gets on by the front door, followed by two men. As if in a dance, they pass her in the aisle to the right and left, the bus is still standing there with its motor running, waiting, the woman sees the men and at once tries to turn around and run back out the front door, but the men grab her by the hair, the woman begins to scream, the men drag her toward the back of the bus by the hair, and when the screaming woman now falls down, trying in vain to find a grip somewhere with her hands, and is dragged past us, her limbs contorted, my wet-nurse starts shouting: Not by the hair! For pity's sake, not by the hair! But the men seem not to hear what my wet-nurse is shouting, and then I see how this woman, who doesn't want to follow the men and therefore has stopped moving her feet but is nonetheless inextricably joined to her hair, falls out of the bus through one of the back doors right into the arms of the men, who have gotten out before her, and only now does the bell ring, giving the usual signal that the bus is about to depart, to warn anyone who might be intending to get on or off of the closing doors, the sound of the bell mingles with the woman's screams, which become fainter and eventually inaudible as the bus shuts its doors and resumes its route. Only then do I notice that blood is dripping from my nose onto my pink checked dress, my wet-nurse says, we'll wash it out when we get home, with cold water.

On the way home, I tip my head back and try to stem the flow of blood with a handkerchief, I look up and see the sky, my wet-nurse is leading me by the hand to keep me from falling, she says: Careful, a curb, wait, there's a car coming on the right, here's a little dog. I know that beneath my shoes is the smooth, shiny pavement of the city in which I live, stone islands: black, gray and white, but all I see are clouds, distant water drifting past, it almost never rains here, my wet-nurse pulls me to her by the elbow and says: Watch out, a beetle. I stare at the sun, blind today to the large, steaming cup that has been set into the ground here, a mosaic of paving-stones on the sidewalk of the big street on the rounded corner where the café is, just a few blocks from our garden. I hear the voices of the people sitting here, hear them turning the pages of their newspapers, my gaze burned white by the sun. We turn to the left. Radio music is coming out of the shop where my mother always brings shoes for repair, I know that the metal roller blinds have been let down, see the sky and know that the shop is nonetheless open and that the owner is sitting in its most shadowy corner at a large machine that smells of oil, waiting for customers. I see an airplane high up in the sky, see it before I can hear it, see the white streak it carves into the blue, my parents are up there, they're on their way to Alaska, or: That's my mother's airplane, she's traveling to Rome, or: Today my father's sitting in that plane up there, he's flying far far away, where's he going, really far away, well if you don't even know where he's going then it can't be true, yes it is, my father's even flying across the ocean, well so where's he going. Mangos and oranges and strawberries, a sweet smell, for ten paces the sky is closer to me and bears green and yellow stripes, the awning is a roof for fruit and shoppers, the grocer cranks it out of the wall every day after lunch, or has the fruit already been spoiled by the sun, does it smell rotten, oh no, my wet-nurse says, it looks nice and is in the shade. A few steps further, children are quarrelling on the steps of the ice-cream shop over a few coins, today I can't even buy you an ice-cream, my wet-nurse says, and guides my feet to the right to where it is quieter, our street. Before our garden gate, we detour around the man who is burning the grass from beneath the paving stones. I can't see the piece of equipment he's using, just hear its hoarse flickering sound. No, I say, but how about tomorrow.

When because of the blood still flowing from my nose my mother holds my face under cold water until it turns to stone—my wet-nurse has meanwhile set to work on the pink checked dress—but even at other times, when my mother rips a bandage from my knee with an abrupt jerk, or combs my hair with a comb that gets stuck in it and then says to me: Really, your hair, or when she shows me how to pull a pair of thin stockings over my legs, pinching my leg along with the stockings, at such moments I'd like to see her fall down the stairs or out the window, see her accidentally stab herself while slicing bread. Whenever she says: It's just going to hurt for a second, then it'll feel better, or: I know it pinches a little, but you're a big girl now. You have to suffer for beauty, she says. Beauty, beauty, a rat in your guts, your head in the cesspool, beauty. Every time my mother hurts me, just for a second, a tiny little bit, it won't last long, be brave, I always want to see her head spinning away from me, reverberating with the good hard slap I've just given her, and at last she'll be still.

Father, I say, they just came and took the woman away. We are sitting on the living room rug, I am busy cutting the letters of the alphabet out of fuzzy black paper for school, my father squats beside me on the rug, sorting the letters I've cut out into words. And even though my wet-nurse asked them not to pull the woman's hair, they dragged her out of the bus by the hair. I see, my father says. In the kitchen next door, Mother is frying things, washing lettuce, stirring and chopping. What were you doing in that neighborhood in the first place. The words long live are written in black on our carpet. It was because of the Difunta, I say. Who's that, my father asks. A saint, I say, there's an altar to her there. I see, my father says. Why do you think those men took the woman away, I ask my father. Jealousy, he says, betrayal, love—they must have had some reason. Do you think she's all right now? I'm sure she is, my father says.

Yesterday the railway workers tried to shoot out the tires of all the buses. The railway workers? I ask Anna. Yes, she says, didn't you hear the shots. Uh-huh, I say. So because of this it is forbidden, starting today, to travel by train. Oh, I say. Starting today, my friend says, there'll be a market in the station and on the tracks.

We could buy the shoes there, I say to my wet-nurse. The shoe shop where we usually pick out shoes for her is closed today for technical reasons. In this shop, I alway used to play hide-and-seek with Marie, my wet-nurse's daughter, who in fact is my milk sister, behind the mirrors propped up at angles, while my wet-nurse was pulling various shoes onto her bony faerie feet and then walking up and down a few steps to see which ones fit. My wet-nurse stands for a long time studying the notice affixed to the closed blinds of the shop, which does not make it clear whether the shop is to be closed today only or perhaps tomorrow as well, but Marie has already seized me by the hand and is tugging me off in the direction of the train station.

When I see how shabby the station's cupola suddenly looks, I feel surprised at how quickly real life has taken note of the ban. Large pieces of cloth have been hung up to keep the plaster from falling on people's heads. Merchants have already set up shop in the ticket windows and on the platforms, they are selling handbags or scarves, candy, electrical cable, flowers and appliances. It is difficult to see the tracks between these plies of goods for sale, only occasionally does it happen that you are gazing at sneakers and watches and your eyes suddenly slip down into a gravel-filled crevice and off into the distance. You can still always just walk where you want to go. The shoes are inexpensive.

It's much faster to go by car anyhow, my father says. But: The smell of iron, the smeared windowpanes, the toilet with piss on the floor, when I flushed I could see the earth flying past beneath me through a hole, stepping from one car to the next, always with the fear the train might split in two, strangers putting bread and eggs into their mouths and audibly chewing, seats that could be transformed by skillful hands into beds, sleeping on the train, dreaming in the rhythm of the crossties, then waking up and being there already. When I get home, I'll have to get the old picture books down from the attic and cut out the locomotives, steam, conductor and all.

We have to drive far into the countryside to visit my father's parents. There never used to be altars beside the railway tracks because no one traveled on foot there. But from the back seat of the car I now and then see heaps of bottles filled with water, transparent mountains in honor of the Difunta. My mother says, how uncouth, unloading garbage in the countryside like that. My father says, it's time for things to be put in order around here. My parents hand me a bottle of water. I drink. Car.

Once a year we go to visit my father's parents. We always spend four days with them during Pentecost. My grandmother has a high, rapid way of speaking, a child's voice, and for a long time I was convinced that every one of the little curls clinging tightly to her head was one of her words. My grandfather has a great deal of strength. When he says hello to me, he always starts by squeezing my hand in such a way that the ring I wear, a gift from my wet-nurse, leaves bright red marks on the fingers to either side. Then he pulls me to him by one hand and wraps his arms around me, his embrace always makes me think of the machine belonging to the man who repairs our shoes in the shadowy corner of his shop, being embraced by my grandfather makes me feel like a shoe being inserted into this machine, and sooner or later, I assume, this rough treatment will tear the ears from my head.

My grandfather is a businessman. In the city in which my father was a child, I have never seen a single person who did not respond in kind when my grandfather greeted him. He's in real estate, my father says, and there's scarcely a building or piece of land here that did not at some point pass through his hands. It wouldn't be so surprising, I think, if my grandfather's hands, which grasp and release buildings and properties on a daily basis, were accidentally to tear off a little girl's ear some day. Do you know, my father's mother says to me with her curly little voice, I'm just setting the table while she reads the newspaper, do you know, she says, peering over the newspaper so she can observe me, how well-off you are with your parents. Yes, I say. You'd have to look far and wide to find parents like that, she says, and waits to see how I'll respond. I say: I know, and go to the cupboard to get out the cutlery. In the afternoon, when I'm just darting into the kitchen from the garden to get a drink, the living room door is slightly ajar and I hear my grandmother inside saying to my grandfather with her curlicue voice: There's something inherently spoiled about her, she'll always be like that, regardless of upbringing. And my grandfather's response: You may be right. Perhaps that's why he wants to tear my ears off, so I won't hear him and his wife talking about me in secret. On Pentecost, the disciples spoke to each man in his own tongue, my father told me as we were traveling to see his parents, by car this year for the first time. Each one of them was able to understand the word of God. And where was Jesus on Pentecost? Jesus had already died and been resurrected. What does a person look like when he's been resurrected, I ask. Just like always, he says, except now you can't grab hold of him. But ever since then languages have been separate again, I ask. Yes, my father says. I remember this conversation when I hear my grandparents speaking poorly of me through the living room door the Saturday before Pentecost.

The pews on which my father sat when he was a child are narrow and hard. Jesus is nailed to the cross up in front. *In the beginning was the word*, the man standing in the pulpit says. My grandmother is gazing at the speaker, her eyes shining, each of her little curls wide awake, while my grandfather seems to be staring right through the wall of the church and grinding something massive with his iron jaws, perhaps he's clearing land in his thoughts. My father is holding my hand, my mother with her eyes the color of water is suddenly a foreigner in this nave, the innermost core of our nation, she lowers her eyes and during the entire sermon keeps them fixed on her blue leather handbag which is hanging from a hook beneath the shelf for the hymnal, a gift from my father. Up in front, Jesus is nailed to the cross. The man in the pulpit is telling the story of Creation, and if I understand correctly, what happened was that reality filled God's words to the brim with all the things God spoke of when he still had no one to talk to but himself: The trees grew into his word tree, the fish swam after his word fish and quickly slipped into it between scales that were already there from his speaking of scales, the birds darted up to the sky, following the feathers God had already proclaimed, and pulled them on over their heads, and Adam and Eve filled the words Adam and Eve with blood, bones, kidneys, intestines, heart, eyes and mouth and all the rest of what God talked about to himself when he was still alone. You'd have to look far and wide to find parents like that. Up in front, Jesus is nailed to the cross. Why does mankind have so many different languages? I ask my father as we are walking back to his parents' house hand in hand after the service. So now can anyone just come and take a word away from the thing it belongs to, I ask, or toss it over some other thing like a blanket, can any person who speaks be a thief? Can he? And what about a person who keeps silent? Do you need the word chair to sit in a chair? No, I say. Well then, my father says. And if a person says, I am sitting, and you can see he is stand, ing up, do you need the word chair? No, I say. You don't have to speak of things you can grab hold of. But then what about the ones who were resurrected, I want to ask, but just then we reach my grandparents' house and my father is holding the door for everyone. There's something inherently spoiled about her, my grandparents said when they thought I wouldn't hear them. Perhaps it's because the railway has been abolished that you can no longer ride along the words as if they were tracks, always arriving at the same thing by the same route. Only recently, since we've started going places on foot or in the car, have I begun to notice forks in the road again, crossroads, or old and new roads leading in the same direction by parallel paths, and also regions that don't have any roads at all, but even then you can still get places by walking as the crow flies. Since the railway has been abolished, words can run away from their things in all sorts of ways, they can hide in the underbrush or the mountains. Trees, fish and birds stand in silence somewhere while someone who possibly has never seen them before is talking about them, or someone who has seen them neglects to bring them up. In front of the church, on the cross, Jesus is nailed. Pews, tablecloths, green twigs, Jesus on the cross, his body contorted, the pulpit whose roof is heavily laden with wooden fruits and leaves, the hook on which you can hang your handbag, shining eyes, jaws made of iron, my father's warm hand, my mother's eyes the color of water that she is trying to conceal, and Jesus, who always and everywhere, in every church, but also in the street, in public squares and courtyards, in rooms, corners, niches and above people's beds is fastened firmly to the cross. God must have been terribly lonely before he began with Creation, otherwise a person doesn't speak to himself of kidneys and bones.

The Difunta walked right through the desert without a path, I say to my wet-nurse when we're back from our Pentecost trip, the two of us are walking on the shady side of the street, my mother's sent us to the market hall to do the shopping. With every step she was able to decide what direction to walk in, and still the only place she got to was her own death. Meat, fish and vegetables, this fresh and at the same time raw smell, and running beneath all of it, an undercurrent, the smell of the rotten produce that is stacked in baskets behind the hall in the mornings and collected in the afternoons. She was free to choose anything at all, but nonetheless she arrived precisely at the place where she would die, I say to my wet-nurse. Every time we come to the market hall, I look at the leaves that have been torn from the turnips and cabbages, all soft beneath my steps, already crushed black by other feet, and feel surprised at how quickly it happens that something that was still alive just a day before can turn rotten and smell bad. It was too long a trip for her, but she couldn't know that beforehand, my wet-nurse says. Today I perceive the smell of rotting food more sharply, today, it seems to me, this smell is overpowering that of the living things, the freshly slaughtered meat and freshly caught fish. If the desert hadn't been so endless, she wouldn't have walked herself to death, my wet-nurse says. Things could have turned out quite differently. Everything you see here wants to be bought, she often used to say to me when we went shopping in the market hall, and then I imagined the fish, pieces of meat and vegetables calling out to the customers until each item, or almost each, had been purchased. In this market hall I realized for the first time that I live in a very large city. If there had been paths, surely she would have encountered some other person who would have been able to give her and her child something to drink, I say to my wet-nurse. We buy apples, grapes and potatoes. Not until we are about to say goodbye in front of my house, and she is handing me the basket, does she say to me: Marie didn't come home. She hasn't been home in three days. Before I can answer, she turns around and leaves, and it seems to me as if I am seeing her back for the first time. You forgot the onions, my mother says when I set down the basket in front of her, didn't you look at the list I gave you.

My father takes me on his lap. I lay myself flat against his belly and curl myself up so that my head comes to rest between his head and shoulder. He rocks me back and forth, softly singing the song of our homeland, a song in a minor key, my and my father's song, we often sit together like this, but while he is really singing, I release my breath only on certain notes, as the desire strikes me, very softly. Sometimes my breath fits with what he is singing, but often it doesn't, and then the whole thing sounds off-kilter and clashes, but this too pleases him and me. I sing him my notes quietly against his skin from the outside, into his throat, while at the same time I am listening through shirt and shoulder to the blood circulating inside my father. Again.

Don't touch, my mother says, can't you see it's wild. The dog I want to pet has been trotting beside me ever since the café on the corner. He just appeared from nowhere, perhaps from the smoke made of stone coming out of the coffee cup set in the ground as a mosaic. The café has been closed for several days. Dog. Just look at it, it's filthy, my mother says. The dog remains at my side. It doesn't even have a collar, my mother says. It's true, the dog doesn't have a collar or a leash. Who do you think would take away even the collar and leash of a dog like that, I ask my mother. It never had a collar and leash, my mother says, you can see it was always wild, it just came to the city out of greed, to eat garbage. It should be put to sleep, my mother says. They multiply just like rats, she says, they come to the city, eat their fill, and then multiply like rats. I let go of my mother's hand and say to the dog: Sit! My mother says, come on, we have to go, the dog sits down. My mother says: Well, then don't, and goes on walking. Lie down! I say to the dog, and the dog lies down. I run after my mother, the dog obeys me, I shout, did you see that. Of course, she says and takes my hand again. A few times I turn around to look at the dog, he is still lying there just where I told him to.

Why am I never allowed to go anywhere by myself, I ask my mother. Because you can never know what might happen, my mother says. We walk into the park at whose center a large man made of stone is standing. Besides this man, no one is here, but in a country where the sun is almost always shining, no one likes to go for walks in the middle of the day, not even in the shade. Or does everyone who comes here alone for a walk get turned to stone, I ask my mother. What nonsense, she replies and goes on walking.

You told your father about our outing, didn't you, my wet-nurse asks me and smiles. She has come to say goodbye to me. Yes, I say. Just imagine, I say, he never heard of the Difunta. Well, he knows other things, my wet-nurse says and smiles. Of course he does, I reply. My father knows all about currents. Let your parents know, my wet-nurse says, tell them that even though I didn't know this before I am seriously ill and cannot work any more. What do you have? I ask. Tell them I have to look after my old father, who lives outside our city. Where does your father live? Tell them I think it would do you good to start finding your own way without me. I see, I say. Then she gets up, gives me a hug, still smiling, and leaves. When I look out the window to watch her go, I see the olive-colored handbag from which she one day retrieved the little card with the picture of the Difunta dangling from her arm, just the way it used to on all our walks.

Certain things are now being centrally regulated, my father says when I tell him that the coffee cup on the corner where the café used to be now has a beard of grass, as does the steam made of stone rising from it. As you see, he says, the café didn't make it. That's true, I think, for in the last few weeks before it closed, I saw fewer and fewer people sitting there. They were really cutthroat businessmen, my father says, or do you think people want to give an arm and a leg for a cup of coffee. The city will go to ruin, my father says, if individuals who think only of themselves are allowed to call the shots. The sentence spoken by the examiner at my audition for the music school occurs to me: Only a person who appreciates beauty can make music. And what about the man who always burns the grass away in front of our house? He's on vacation, my father says.

Other people have our piano now, I hear someone saying behind me as I am just about to shut the window because it's already so hot again outside. I turn around and see the red-haired girl who didn't pass the audition for the music school sitting on my sofa, her legs are dangling down and are still so short that even if this girl were able to play the piano, she'd never be able to reach the pedals. How come you haven't grown since then, I want to ask, but just then the door quietly opens and the housekeeper serves us cookies on a plate. I thought you girls would like these, she says and smiles, then she leaves us alone again. Even the table where I learned to write, the girl says. And my mother's crystal collection. When the girl stands up now to hand me the plate, there isn't even an imprint from her body left behind on the sofa, that's apparently how little she weighs.

Your father works hard, my mother says. No cars to the left, no cars to the right, then hurry across. We are picking my father up from work, just like every Friday. In the building in which my father keeps everything in order the grass is probably up to his knees by now. He's got to slash his way through with a knife, and when finally he's found order and wants to give it something to eat and drink, it lashes out at him, biting and scratching, order is ungrateful. There are many in this city who fail to appreciate beauty, many who do not value the gift that has been given them and allow the thing entrusted them to deteriorate. It's work to be human, my father once said, and I myself can see how nature reclaims everything that isn't defended against it day after day. To keep the sea from sweeping it into the sea. Certain things are now being centrally regulated, my father said, this is a transitional period, we are setting out upon new paths. We are going where no one has gone before us. A person who wants to sell his car parks it beside the road with an empty bottle on its roof. I know that the city's stone carpet patterns are beneath my feet, gray, black and white, I used to leap from island to island when I went out with my mother: Those who. Then their friends. The ones who remember. Who are afraid. And finally everyone. Always black or always white or always gray, holding my mother's hand. New paths. The grass has already begun to obscure the black, white and gray. Green. Now I can walk straight ahead, right through the islands and the sea. Setting out upon new paths, where no one has walked before. Where the grass is growing. My father knows all about currents. Work.

If my wet-nurse were here now, I could ask her why there wasn't any grass growing in the desert where the Difunta was walking. After all, the Difunta too had chosen a path no one had walked before. Or had so many people already walked there that all the grass was trampled? Is that what they call a desert? But then all of them must have been gone already by the time the Difunta passed by, otherwise someone would have found the saint before she died of thirst. Wouldn't they have? My father, my father. In other countries in which there is a time of year when snow covers everything, a person whose job it is to keep everything in order might possibly be able to take a rest, but here, where the sun is always shining, everything is constantly growing, everything simultaneously blossoms, bears fruit and sheds leaves without pause. Except in the desert. In the desert my father could rest from his labors.

I'm so glad to see you, I say to Marie, my wet-nurse's daughter. My mother never used to allow her to come to our house, but today I walk into my room and there she is standing at the window gazing at the mountain. I see Marie, and at the same time I look right through her at the mountain, and the mountain, for which the window-frame was always too tight a fit, now has plenty of room inside Marie's body. I pull a chair up to the table so she can sit down beside me, there's already a plate of cake there. Your housekeeper brought it for me, Marie says. But eating isn't so easy for me anymore, she says, and only now, when she turns around, do I see she no longer has any hands, they've been cut off just above the wrist. Marie sits down next to me and hides her incomplete arms in her lap as if she were ashamed of them. I don't know whether the shoebox with the hands fell on the grass or into the flower-bed, she says. When I go to stroke her head, there's nothing but air.

But if you prune them daily, they can grow to be two hundred years old, my mother says, taking the shears back from me against my will and using them to indicate her little trees which are no taller than a head of cabbage. Because they have to concentrate more on growing. My mother has never taken any interest in our garden, instead she has always collected these landscapes that you can place on the windowsill in large clay bowls, landscapes in which the boulders are the size of pebbles and the trees are all knotted and twisted because they can't go straight up. The resistance challenges them, my mother says. And because of this there is more strength in each of these dwarf trunks than in an entire forest simply growing without any help from humankind.

Think how hard things must have been for her with such a husband, and now this, my mother says to her brother, my uncle. The wife of my uncle, my aunt by marriage, says: If she sells her car, she can pay for the funeral on her own. We ought at least to offer to take her in, my mother says, after all she's our sister. She won't want that, my aunt says. My mother's brother, my uncle, says: How awful it must have been for her, after all she was standing right beside him. And nothing happened to her? I ask. Absolutely nothing, my father says. A miracle, my grandmother says. My mother says: Not a hair on her head was touched. So there was room for a miracle again, I think, because this uncle who lived far away and was married to my mother's older sister died alone. A car went off the road and ran over him on the sidewalk. Perhaps there was snow on the ground there, in the southernmost tip of our country, where I've never been. And that's why the car slipped off the road. Our country is larger than you can imagine. The driver was probably drunk, my grandmother says. My mother's sister, my aunt who lived far away, had been walking arm in arm with her husband, but only he was struck by the car and dragged along the ground a short distance, then he remained lying there and died. Knowing her, she won't even want us at the funeral, says my aunt by marriage. My grandmother says: I'm going to go in any case. I saw my faraway aunt, who is now a widow, and my uncle by marriage, who from one minute to the next was snatched from her side, on only a single occasion. The two of them came to visit only once, for my grandmother's eightieth birthday, when she'd asked to have all her children around her once more. I remember this uncle very clearly, he always said a great many things which caused the other side—my mother, my father, my mother's brother, my aunt by marriage and even my grandmother—to respond with a great deal of silence. I can't remember specifically what this uncle used to say, just a single sentence that kept returning again and again like a refrain and provided the conclusion to whatever train of thought he was pursuing: And this is quite simply not true, it's simply not how it is, he would say from time to time, and afterwards would seem to be awaiting a response. But I think it was precisely this sentence that always produced the silence on the part of the others, a silence that was new to me. The wife of this very talkative uncle, my mother's older sister, was also silent, but in a different way. She was silent at her husband's side and thus seemed to be standing up to the silence of her relatives. Perhaps it was only because of all this silence that paid us a visit on my grandmother's eightieth birthday that I came to believe that my aunt and her husband, who now is no longer alive, had settled in a region of our country in which there is snow. Perhaps this really is why the car ran off the road. It certainly isn't proper to drink in the morning, my aunt now says, but my grandmother doesn't respond.

Anyone who wants is now permitted to shoot pigeons, Anna says, as a series of shots rings out once again beyond the walls of our schoolyard. Because they destroy buildings with their shit. That's a filthy word, I say. But that's the reason, Anna says. And dogs. The wild ones. Sit, I think. Lie down. They multiply just like rats, I say to Anna. That's stupid, Anna says.

Since my piano lesson was cancelled today: the teacher wasn't already sitting on a chair at the piano when I came into the room, the part in her hair wasn't being mirrored in the shiny black of the instrument, she wasn't leafing through her sheet music and didn't nod to me, nor did her eyes narrow to slits, as her smile wasn't there, and so she didn't shake hands with me either, for I didn't even walk over to the piano when I saw there was no one in the lesson room, but instead remained standing at the door for a moment, then quickly turned around and closed the double door from the outside; since my piano lesson was cancelled today, I sit in the tall grass on the lawn in front of the building, waiting for my mother, who will come in an hour to pick me up, my mother uses the hour during which I have my piano lesson to get her hair done, or her finger- or toenails, she lies down on a bench at the salon and gets a tan or a massage. In the middle of the lawn where I am sitting, amid the blossoming grasses which haven't been mowed for some time now, the gardener is on vacation, my father said, amid the stinging nettles and horsetail that are beginning to take over, stands a man made of stone who must also have come alone to take a walk here, I think, and I lean my back against the stone leg of his trousers while I wait. The man is cold. But at least, I think, he was turned to stone while standing up, so that even if the grass were to grow much taller, you would still be able to see him for quite some time. The Difunta died lying down. If she were lying here with her child, it would already be impossible for anyone to find them.

You should be proud—after all, you know him, my mother says. And for the first time I gaze up past the stone trouser legs, let my eyes meander up the stone to the lapels and then to the face that is so smoothly polished a blade of grass could never get caught there and put down roots. And indeed: I see a bowl made of hair that is now made of stone containing the head of the man who not long ago was sitting with us. I think of the Difunta, think of Jesus who everywhere, in every church, but also on streets, public squares and courtyards, in rooms, corners, niches and above people's beds, is forever nailed to the cross, and I ask my mother what the man died of in whose body our food was transformed not long ago into walking and coughing. But my mother says he isn't dead, he's coming to visit us again next Sunday, and then I can ask him myself what it's like to be hewn in stone. I'm definitely not going to shake hands with him again, I think. Shake hands, shake hands, say hello. I don't know whether the box with the hands… So where's the miracle then? My mother says, forget about miracles, superstition can take you only so far, the main thing is having a role model. As we are walking back through the park, this time I raise my eyes at this end, too, where the other man made of stone is standing, and let my eyes travel along the granite placket of a lab coat and up to the head, when I was sick the coat was white, now it's made of reddish granite, the head is as bare as it was when I was sick, and polished smooth as a mirror, perhaps the bald head bending over my sickbed was stone even then and the transformation had already begun imperceptibly from above. You are at home in this city more than others are, my mother says. I can see this. The city is starting to become our own stone dwelling, inhabited by my father's chiseled friends. Everyone should model themselves on these men, my mother says, but at our house they are regular guests. Is everyone who models himself on them supposed to become cold just like them? You are able to see them close up, my mother says, that's something to be proud of. On the median of the main street that leads up the hill, we encounter a third figure made of stone, one which has only recently been erected there. Its face has not yet been carved, but I consider it quite possible that just a few days from now the stone will have soft lips like the lips of a woman. Those who. Then their friends. Those who remember. Who are afraid. And finally everyone. Everyone everyone.

The teacher pulls a ruler out of Anna's pencil case, holds it up in the air and says: Down with the centimeter! And snaps the ruler in two. The smallest new unit of measure is approximately three and a half centimeters long. Electricity, too, has started coming out of the outlet at a faster rate. If a person were now to go on a journey, he would need adaptors to translate the electrical current, but why would anyone want to go traveling outside the country? Our country is larger than I can imagine. Before and Elsewhere are squatting one atop the other, copulating. How disgusting, the teacher says. Milk is now being sold in rectangular cardboard boxes that hold as much liquid as a bucket used to. The teacher says, why should a person go shopping every single day, what use is a mere litre to a large family. Lay in supplies, the teacher says. And then conserve your resources. This is true. But we for example are only father, mother and child. And my mother's brother and his wife are only man and wife. And as of recently, my mother's sister is all alone, a widow. She has surely already placed an empty bottle on the roof of her car to sell it in order to be able to cover the cost of her husband's funeral without assistance. That's an exception, the teacher says. In this country, in which the sun is almost always shining, everything is constantly blossoming, growing and rotting, and young women get pregnant again and again, Anna for example has five siblings, and even if the shooting the other day happened to go well and her sister is no longer alive, that would still leave four. Families like ours are the exception, the teacher says. Perhaps my grandmother brought this withering along with her from the place where my mother was an infant, her face gray and white beneath the woolen cap, brought this dying out from that other world where for several months a year everything lies beneath a layer of snow.

You are our greatest treasure, my father says. You are our greatest treasure, my mother says too. This is one of those sentences where my parents cross paths as if at a busy inter-section. Why don't I have any siblings, I used to ask my mother now and then when I was younger. There are children who have siblings and others who don't, my mother said. My father said: Things might change, you never know. I read somewhere, I say to my mother, that if you cradle a block of wood in your arms long enough and let your tears pour down on it, the block of wood can come to life and turn into either a brother or sister, depending. Who writes nonsense like that, my mother says. Neither my mother's brother nor her faraway sister, who surely has placed the empty bottle atop her car by now, produced children. But my mother is responsible for the existence of a child. The fruit of love. My father no doubt sat there waiting for me to ripen, then he plucked me from the tree and handed me to my mother, and she bit into me just like an apple. Or like... My father is responsible for the existence of a child. Things might change, you never know. My mother's treasure—me—has meanwhile been almost entirely eaten up, and there are no second helpings, or like... My mother is conserving me. Careful, it's hot. My father could keep plucking apples from trees, since the land belongs to him. At least as long as the tree still bears fruit. My mother: the one who boiled me for preserves. My father: the trickster. Whom did the land used to belong to, I ask. A profiteer, my father says, a person who just wanted to make money with his property, you ought to have seen the garden, my father says, the grass was up to your knees. Now the grass everywhere in the city is up to your knees except in our garden, where it is shorn low to the ground, my father has been cutting it himself since the gardener left for vacation. And no one had pruned the fruit trees in years. No one would have wanted to eat the apples that were growing then, my father says, they were small, pulpy and sour. Now not only the apples but all the other fruits of our garden are juicy and sweet, my father plucks them from the tree, then my mother cooks them down to make preserves and seals them in air-tight jars. Lay in supplies and conserve them. You are our greatest treasure. My parents cross paths in this sentence as if at a busy intersection. My father made my mother the gift of a child. Or if need be, saw down the tree, chop it into bits and cry a great deal over it. Careful it's hot. For there are some who do not know how to appreciate it when they are given a gift. Brother and sister. Neither brother nor sister. Neither. Nor. Things might change, you never know.

Even the method of telling time is now different, we are told. Clocks are made by people, are they not, the teacher says. In such a large country as ours, he says, where here everything is blossoming, growing and bearing fruit at the very same time as, in other, more distant regions, it is freezing, snowing or thawing, the concept of "spring" is simply a matter of convention. The only question, he says, is what one wishes to remember and how often. I want to remember my birthday, for example, I say. One day out of all the days of the year is my birthday. One day out of all the days of the year is the day on which I was born. Good, let's take your birthday, the teacher says. Formerly a year had three hundred and sixty-five days, did it not, he says. Yes, I say. And after three hundred and sixty-five days, you punctually feel in the mood for your birthday. Yes, I say. And what do you do when it's leap year, the teacher asks. Does your feeling persist one day longer? I don't know, I say. And what would you do if you were to lose your calendar or sleep through an entire day and you no longer knew what time it was? Then my parents would come in with the table covered with presents and the music box. I see, the teacher says. But if your parents were to come into your room with the table after only two hundred and fifty days, or not until five hundred and twenty-seven, would you enjoy your presents any less? No, I say. Well then, the teacher says. All these things are a matter of convention. You cannot feel time, he says. Time has to be measured. Clocks, after all, are made by people and not the other way around.

My father-in-law doesn't see well, our housekeeper says. Last week he didn't even want to come to the movies with me, she says. My mother says: I'm sorry to hear that. Our housekeeper says: The sunlight is hard on him. What he likes best is to sit with all the shades drawn, and he doesn't even listen to the radio anymore. He just sits there. My mother says: The hallway needs mopping. Okay, the housekeeper says, gives me a smile and puts on her rubber gloves.

If my wet-nurse were here, I'd ask her about the sun. Day and night still exist, even here, in this country where at least during the day the sun is almost always shining. Our house-keeper says her father-in-law couldn't care less whether it's night or day. When she brings him his breakfast, then it's morning, her father-in-law says to her, and that's good enough for him. When a person stays sitting in the dark too long, the day has only twenty-three hours. For example. That's what my father says. My father knows all about currents. When a person is put into a niche overnight that is sealed up in front with a door, in the morning he'll fall out like a board.

I'm sitting on the steps in front of our house, I forgot my key. The young man who listened to me play the piano not long ago is sitting next to me, smoking a cigarette. Do you like living here, he asks. Yes, I say. Sometimes it surprises me, he says, how little about a house is actually the house itself. You can see that when there are lights on inside, he says, and takes a drag on his cigarette. Basically, all houses are transparent, the young man says, but when you are sitting inside, you don't notice, probably because the furniture and the rugs and all the things hanging on the walls block your view of the air. I can't help thinking of the glass bones of our housekeeper, who wears her aprons tied ever so tightly about her waist. Perhaps it's the same with her: she'd be transparent if she walked around without an apron. When I see a house from the outside at night, the young man says to me, it always surprises me a little that it isn't collapsing with all the heavy furniture in it. In our house there is a great deal of heavy furniture, I think, the older I get the more there is, my parents have been collecting old furniture as long as I can remember, they say it's nice for things finally to be given a place appropriate to their quality, to have a home where they are valued. Walls are basically as thin as paper, the young man says, thinner than the shells of shrimp. You are our greatest treasure. The young man sits next to me, smoking in silence. Whenever the priest talked about Noah's ark on Sundays, I always imagined the rooms of our house: cupboards, highboys and gothic benches, chandeliers, rugs, mirrors and pictures that took refuge here as if from a great flood. Where did this piece of furniture use to be, I ask my father as he instructs the workmen carrying a white and gold armoire into our front hall. My father says: You won't believe it, but I found this one in a pigsty, it was being used to store the fodder. On top of the cupboard two angels are trumpeting. Before I am allowed to place my sweaters inside it, my mother takes a hand brush and dustpan and cleans out the shelves. Food for animals, she says, in a genuine Baroque armoire. All I can see is dust. And when a person wants to eat a shrimp, the young man says, he just peels it out of its shell. With his bare hands, he says. Pink-colored walls, and the pink already flaking. Alas, the young man says and now falls silent as he sees my father coming toward us through the garden gate, my father gives me his hand and helps me to my feet, then he kisses me and says: So were you very bored, that's all he says, he just goes on ahead to open the door for me, goes up the steps, walking right through the feet, knees and heart of the young man, who has remained seated there, my father unlocks the door and stands to one side to let me go in before him, then he follows and shuts the door behind us, now we are in the cool interior of the house. Outside the man is no doubt still sitting there smoking his cigarette, outside the sun is no doubt still shining, just the same as ever.

My little sister finally came home yesterday, Anna says. That's nice, I say. She went right upstairs, Anna says, to our parents' bedroom, to the wardrobe, and took the air pistol out of the compartment where my father always keeps his handkerchiefs. Our parents hid it under their linens so we wouldn't find it, Anna says. My little sister, Anna says, took the air pistol out of its compartment, held it to her head and pulled the trigger. How old is your little sister, I ask. She was seven, Anna says.

She didn't even close the door to the wardrobe first, she says to me. I don't say anything. And my parents still aren't home yet, she says. Why not, I ask. First they went on vacation with my little sister, she says, to the mountains, but then a volcano erupted and wiped out the roads, so they had to stay longer than they'd planned to. Then they stopped on the way back to visit our grandparents, and my father was attacked right in front of the house by a rabid wolf, he had to go to the hospital, and on the very same day he was released, my grand⁄mother slipped and fell, and so my parents stayed even longer, my mother kept house for my grandparents for a few weeks and took care of my grandfather, and my father went fishing a lot during this time, he likes to do that, Anna says, there's a lake there, and he caught a pike, they put it in the bathtub still alive and my little sister tamed it, on command it would jump out of the water and back again in a big arc like a dolphin, and finally, when they really were about to come home, the news arrived that they'd won a cruise, a trip around the entire world, they had to board the ship immediately, and so they went from my grandparents' house with their packed suitcases straight to the coast, but first they sent my little sister back home to us. How long have your parents been gone now, I ask. A year or two, Anna says. Oh, I say, I didn't know. And who's been taking care of your family all this time, I ask. First my big sister took care of us, but after she fell in love, I did, Anna says. The Mazurka in F minor is the last piece Chopin wrote. And how much longer will the cruise last? No one knows, Anna says. The world is big, you know. Larger than you can imagine. Yesterday my little sister finally came home, she says. She rang the doorbell right when I got home from school. My mother forgot to give her the key. She didn't have any luggage either. She didn't even say hello, Anna says, she just ran right upstairs into our parents' bedroom, to the wardrobe, and took the air pistol out of the compartment where my father always keeps his handkerchiefs, it was hidden there, and she held it to her head and pulled the trigger. You heard the shot, didn't you, Anna says to me. And she didn't even close the door to the wardrobe first, she says.

Marie is giving the little girl a piggyback ride, you can do that without hands. They ride like that to the window and back again, many trips from the sofa to the window and back. My piano teacher is sitting at the piano, this time she's playing a humorous piece, playing it quickly, faster and faster, probably she's smiling as she plays, but her smile is not reflected in the shiny black of the piano, nor are her hair and shoulders, not even her arms, which are reaching far to the left and right to put some verve into the humorous piece, no, I see only the back of my piano teacher, and through it I see the shiny body of my piano, in which the reflected black and white keys are jumping up and down like mad, Marie begins to gallop, the little girl screeches with pleasure. The little girl looks so much like Anna that I didn't even have to ask her name when she walked into my room. She's tucked the air pistol between her belt and dress so she won't lose it on her ride. Finally Marie unloads her burden on the sofa and falls onto the cushions beside the girl. I'm thirsty! the two of them cry in unison, they close their eyes, laughing, and gasp for breath, but the music keeps going. I run down to the kitchen, everything's quiet down there, my mother is just pruning her kitchen herb garden in the clay pots on the windowsill, she says, why are you so out of breath, are you feverish again, I say I'm fine, our housekeeper puts four glasses and a bottle of mineral water on a tray for me. Finally a bit of life around here, she says and smiles. Uh-huh, I say. My mother asks why I need four glasses, and what sort of life… but at just this moment one of the clay pots cracks apart in her hands and she forgets what she was asking, she curses the soil that's fallen on the floor, the housekeeper goes to get a broom and I leave the kitchen, balancing the tray on my hand all the way up the stairs, always the outer edge of the curve, the steps there are so wide there's room for my whole foot, close to the center I might slip, my mother said when I was little, adding: Careful.

Early in the morning, as we are waiting for the sports festival to begin, the air is still cool, and the smell of jasmine drifts across to us from the dusty bushes at the edge of the field. But as soon as the sun begins scorching the field, one of the teachers fires the starter's pistol, aiming at the sun, you heard the shot, didn't you, Anna says, but the sun doesn't fall out of the sky. From the moment this shot rings out, our bodies are kept moving at a trot from station to station, from one piece of equipment to the next—sweat, drink a lot, complete the circle —from the moment the shot rings out, our bodies are being measured against one another in exercise after exercise. The capacity of our flesh to leap, run, balance, hurl, throw or be thrown is being measured, faster, higher and farther. Knees, arms, heels, thighs and tendons, hair tied back to keep it out of the way. My mother gave me tea to bring with me: sweat, drink a lot, tea without sugar. And fruit. Food is important for a strong mind in a strong body, my aunt likes to say. And what else? Is that it? Just food? *Why oh why did the banana start to fly?* When a head knows how far back it must bend in order to succeed in throwing the discus the hand is holding, does this make it better able to resist the knife about to sever it from its torso? And if not, what happens to the knowledge of throwing that falls out of it? Does it wind up in the basket along with the head? Or does it fly off and go on vacation? My father's up there. My mother. High high up. He or she is now on a flight to Rome. To Rimini. Or Hawaii. The teacher says a sports festival is for celebrating bodies. You have to celebrate holidays on whatever days they happen to fall. Why do holidays fall? Why oh why. *'Cause no one caught its yellow skin and dragged it down to earth again.*

When we run into my wet-nurse on the street—I'm walking beside my mother to what used to be the grocer's shop to collect our rations, the market hall has been closed for months —we say hello to her, and the wet-nurse too utters a greeting, and when my mother says to her that it's been particularly hot these past few days, she says: Yes. My wet-nurse is wearing an olive-colored skirt and brown stockings, and her hair is now gray all over. Sand grates beneath my shoes, someday someone will have to dig up the mosaics if he wants to go hopping through the city on islands of stone, first those, then those, then those, and finally everyone, the sand has gotten caught in the grass that shoots up tall between the paving stones. You heard the shots yourself, didn't you. Why can't I ever go anywhere all by myself. The closed blinds of the shop where my mother once brought our shoes for repair are now dusty. In front of the café on the corner, the lock securing the blinds is already rusted. The street has shut its eyes and is quiet. Silence is health. Well then, my mother says to my wet-nurse. The nurse says: I should be going. Good bye, my mother says first, then I say it, then my wet-nurse.

No. For once let me just set the holidays down and dance, take myself into my own arms and for once just dance, scoop my body from the pit into which I've fallen, spit out the sand, remove my heels from the iron blocks on which they've been propped awaiting the starter's pistol, and hoist myself out of the watery lane marked on either side by a row of corks, let me celebrate my body, but without measuring tape and stop-watch, without sense and reason, dance, move my limbs however the fancy strikes me, simply celebrate that there is something in the place where my flesh and blood are and not nothing, that's how the young woman put it when she came in and hugged me and I felt nothing at all of her hug, as all the others followed her, gradually filling up my room, when if not on my birthday did my flesh and blood belong to me, she asked and then she switched on a little cassette recorder and sat down on the sofa, good music, when if not today should I be allowed, today or some other day, what does it matter, one of all the days in the year is, after all, the day on which I was born, and in any case today we are celebrating my birthday.

This afternoon we are celebrating and dancing while my mother celebrates her own body, either sitting or lying down, celebrates it without moving, my mother always says it's getting to be time for me as well to entrust my hands, feet and hair to someone who knows what to do with them, today, while she is reclining on a couch in one of these salons, entrusting her body or parts of it to someone who knows what to do with them, or else lying down on a tanning bed so as finally to be at home on this shore of the world, to grow into this continent on which the sun is almost always shining, while my piano lesson is not occurring, as has been the case for several weeks now, we are dancing, we dance as my mother puts her body

in strangers' hands, luxuriating, and my father is being visited
by several men, such as the one whose head rests in his beard
as if in a bowl made of hair, also the doctor with the bald
head and one or two others as well who no doubt have also
been hewn in stone by now and are keeping the city cool, we
dance as my father is holding court and the first floor of our
house smells of tobacco although the door to his room remains
tightly closed, these stony men are holding stone, and therefore
everything is perfectly quiet downstairs, for the housekeeper
isn't there either, she's broken one of her glass bones again and
is at home in bed, lying flat on her back, but not to celebrate
her body like my mother, she is merely waiting for the glass to
melt back together again, but her father-in-law is sitting at her
bedside and objects to her letting the sunlight in, so the bone
cannot mend and the housekeeper can't come back to our
house, if the Difunta had broken a glass bone, it wouldn't
have been long before it had melted back together again in the
sun, and while you can't hear a word in our house, and no one
is washing clothes or dishes either, we are celebrating my
birthday upstairs, and dancing because there has been something and not nothing where my body is for so-and-so-many
years now, how many exactly doesn't matter, celebrating my
birthday, although there are a good five months left before
my birthday arrives.

Is this the new system for telling time, I'd asked the young woman when she came into my room without knocking, her hands filled with colorful balloons, but she hadn't replied, after her the young man arrived holding a cake, for a strong mind in a strong body, there were eighteen pink candles burning on it, even though my birthday is five months away and I'm only going to be seventeen, the young man was followed by Anna's sister with red ribbons in her hair, the air pistol stuck in her belt, and Marie without hands, it doesn't matter, one of all the days in the year, after all, is the day on which I was born. The young man placed the cake on my desk, the woman released the balloons to float around the room and put on music, and while the first guests to arrive were still giving me their birthday wishes, new guests were already squeezing into the room. Marie was the first to start dancing. Meanwhile the room has completely filled up with guests, all of them are dancing, they are laughing and dancing and speaking loudly with one another, my piano teacher has come, and even the gardener who has been neglecting his work for so long now, others I know only by sight, for example the cobbler from the shadowy shop on the corner, or the woman who had such long hair when she got on the bus that she could be dragged off by the hair, her hair is gone now, but she is laughing, and when she gets herself a piece of cake, and then another, and then another, I can see all the other guests dancing right through her body, and through the guests standing behind her I can see yet other guests. A boy who not long ago used to go to our school is dancing with Marie, and since she doesn't have hands any longer, he is holding her by the shoulders when it's time for her to spin around. A handful of children including the red-haired girl who flunked the entrance examination are racing back and forth, back and forth with Anna's little sister from sofa to window and from window to sofa and back again, they are balancing eggs on their spoons as they run, and it doesn't matter at all that the room is so full, for the children with their spoons simply run right through the bodies of the dancers, and the young man cheers them on and shouts bravo every time one of them gets to the other side without dropping the egg.

But my father doesn't come upstairs to celebrate with us, and everything is perfectly quiet each time I go down to fetch bottles of mineral water from the refrigerator for my guests, or orange juice for the kids, and later even a bit of wine, everything downstairs remains perfectly still, and my father's door does not open a single time. The footsteps of the dancers cannot be heard at all down here, not even the children screeching or the laughter, but no sounds emanate from my father's room either, as if my father and his visitors were petrified with astonishment at something as yet unknown to me; only from outside, from the street, do I hear something like the roiling of water in which there are a great many fish packed in so tightly they keep bumping together and the water is bubbling and seething with fish and brown from the mud stirred up by them, the water keeps rearing up in countless silvery bodies as if the water itself were a body, nipping at itself and breathing with a thousand wide-open mouths, and in this way, I assume, it is making this sound I have never before heard, that today is striking our house from the outside.

Come, my father says, taking me by the hand, we have to leave. My mother is already sweeping my clothes from the Baroque armoire into a bag. Am I to be nourished on this journey by animal fodder, or by dust. For a strong mind in a strong body. It is nighttime. I am standing at the foot of a ramp made of concrete. So are we going to our uncle's funeral after all, I ask my mother. No, she says. Perhaps this sound I'd never heard before really did come from the great flood, and we are now abandoning this house, which has become too cramped, to all the pieces of furniture, rugs and mirrors that have taken refuge here over time, we are locking the door carefully so as to save the chandeliers, gothic benches, oil paintings and blue-patterned porcelain, and are going outside to drown. Nonsense, my mother says. Or are we going on vacation to visit our gardener? My father says: You're going to see snow. So that's why we're departing in the middle of the night, so the snow won't melt beneath the sun before we get there. Exactly, my father says. Your mother is staying here, he says. Let her fall down the stairs in this house crammed full of objects or get squeezed out the window. You have to suffer for beauty. Before the hands of strangers who know what they are doing can go to work on my skin and hair, my father takes me away.

We drive until we reach the foothills. But before we can get out, the car is surrounded by footsteps, and we see men shining flashlights at us, hear them tapping at the glass with their hands in search of a window that's been left open, my father starts the car again and uses it to thrust the men aside, and then we drive as fast as we can until we reach a place where there are no more men and the road vanishes among the trees, and we keep on driving for quite some time between the trees. At some point we stop, leave the car behind in the forest and begin our climb in a place that has no path. When we look behind us, we can still see tiny circular lights swinging back and forth down below, drunken stars slowly attempting to follow us, and for a while we hear shouts as well. Then it becomes quieter. Completely silent. And eventually, at last, when we have climbed quite high, from one step to the next, there is something bright and cold underfoot. The snow line, my father says. When I turn around, I can now see the shimmering slope marked with the black holes we are making, the prints left by our shoes. As we continue to climb, I claw my fingers through the snow all the way to the rock and look back. Press the keys down as deep as you can and go even deeper once the note has sounded, keep your little finger on its tip, staccato. Count to yourself. When the same note is to be struck more than once, change fingers, but make each attack exactly as strong as the one before. The abyss on the other side is suddenly right before me, I'd almost gone headfirst over the edge, downhill much faster than up. This side, that side. Now come this way, my father says, pointing to the left. The path he is showing me is so narrow you can put your feet down only in single file, and from the way we came it slopes down just as steeply as on the other side, the valleys are invisible from here, they have gotten stuck somewhere in the night far far below us, where it is still too warm for snow. I can't walk here. You have to, my father says. Haven't you ever walked along a mountain ridge, the young woman asks me, she is balancing very skillfully, without slipping, on the steep slope to my right. No, I say. We have to, my father says to me. All you have to do is not look down, the young woman says, then it's perfectly easy. It's perfectly easy, I say to my father. You see, he says, and keeps walking in front of me without turning around. I keep my eyes on his heels.

Surrounding us is a room filled with shadows, its door ajar, the lock was already broken open before we got there, the door leads to a garden that's gone to seed, and on the other side of the garden, where the land slopes down steeply behind the bushes, is the sea. All sorts of other things lie beyond the sea. But just the way my father took the song of our homeland, which I'd always heard trumpeted out of loudspeaker boxes on the street, and made it small and soft for me and combined it with my breath, all the huge vastness we left behind us as we fled is becoming small and soft as well, and as soon as I reach my father's lap, it leaps into his arms.

You know, my father says, everyone who comes to us has to go through the same thing. There has to be some justice. Yes, I say, of course. We certainly cannot demand of one person, he says, that he tell the truth, and then not ask the same thing of another. No, I say. The most important things for starters, says my father, are heat, cold and wet. Heat, cold and wet. Because all the things a person's ever thought are still present in his flesh. To begin with, you have to soften the flesh. Heat, cold or wet for the body of the person who has committed an offense, and at the same time send his gaze down a cul-de-sac, my father says, that's how you begin to guide his concentration to what is most crucial. To what is crucial, the offense, to delinquency and deliquescence, the things that fade away and rot. Precisely, my father says, so we start off with heat, cold or wet, and then you've got to have at least panes of milk glass to block off the windows, if there are windows at all, or better yet, brick over any hole that might let in some light. Paradise was an island too, my father says. And the person on duty is God. Precisely, my father says. *Be present at our table, Lord, be here and everywhere adored.* And now, he says, there are various approaches to choose from. Good, I say. First, my father says, the body is anchored by the limbs or else hung up by them, on a cot or chair or hook, so that the places most susceptible to pain are easily accessible. For it is only through pain, my father says, that the truth can be brought to light in the case of obstinate subjects. Yes, I say. The best place to bring the truth to light is the same for both men and women, between the legs. Oh, I say. You are no longer a child, my father says. No, I say. But there are other places as well, my father says: the tongue, nipples or eyes, for example. Tongue, nipples or eyes. Also the nape of the neck. The nape of the neck. So now, my father says, when the body has been fixed in place and can no longer escape, you can connect one or several of these places to an electrical circuit, or else, my father says, take up a rod with current running through it and use it to probe, stab or beat the body. Probe, stab or beat. You've seen the iron rod I stick in the ground to drive out the earthworms, haven't you. Yes, I say. Don't stick your fingers up your nose. Imagine something like that, my father says. The electricity drives the worms out of the ground, and the stronger the current, the faster they come out. Anna's father caught a pike the size of a dolphin, do you think he used a rod like that? Probably he did, my father says. So once you've connected a body to the electrical circuit, the truth comes out of it like a worm. That's right, my father says. A strong mind in a strong body. How strong the food itself must be. My father says, if someone stubbornly insists on keeping silent, we have to turn up the electricity until his flesh begins to burn. Careful it's hot. Electricity is the best means to drive what a person knows out of his mouth. But what if someone doesn't know anything? But if you are in a room without an electrical outlet, tongs or a knife will work as well. Tongs. Knife. If the knife is sharp enough, you can cut all the way around the soles of a man's or a woman's feet, for example, and then peel back the skin. Each time the body is injured, the recalcitrant spirit shows its face a bit more. Tear out eyeballs or cut off anything that sticks out—ears, noses, hands, feet—crush nipples, twist the entire body or just individual limbs. Simple kicks can work as well, my father says, if you haven't got any tools handy. *Pattycake pattycake baker's man.* If one of them needs longer, take a break with a few vitamins, fresh water, and there's always a doctor in attendance, and then everything starts again from the beginning. Fresh pain in a fresh body. Does the man with the bald head first dispense vitamins and then strike his stony skull against the skull of the obstinate individual until it bursts? If necessary, yes, my father says. Cook the goose of. And in this way the truth comes to light? Usually, my father says. But there are some who refuse to speak even then, my father says. With them, you can forget about the body, you have to go to work quite differently. Strap husband and wife one beside the other on benches. *Man and wife and wife and man, both are part of heaven's plan.* Then a couple of our people on top of the woman who you know, you're not a child any longer. Who know what to do. Or make the husband scream, see above, and the woman is tied up next to him, and make sure she keeps her eyes open, eyes open when you cross the street, to see, or the other way round, and the same thing works with the delinquent's parents, when a person hears through a thin wall for two days, to hear, how in the next room. How in the next room. Hears his father screaming, he'll soon be gagging on the truth and happy to vomit it up. Wait, I say. With little children it's even easier, my father says, starting at a weight of fifty-three pounds they can withstand the electrical current for quite some time. To hear, to see. And then the parents suddenly start talking so fast and so much you can hardly keep up taking notes. Up to fifty-two pounds we do it the other way round, we make the children watch what's happening to their parents. And the doctor weighs the children beforehand? Exactly, my father says, he's always in attendance. *Lullaby and goodnight.* My little sister, says Anna, ran right upstairs to our parents' bedroom, took the air pistol out of the compartment, held it to her head and pulled the trigger. She didn't even close the door to the wardrobe first. So Anna's father and mother are on that on that that sort of cruise. Love serves us well, my father says. Suddenly something crunches underfoot. My grandmother is the only one in the family who can still remember. Your mother's father, your grandfather, whom you never met, used to toss children into the air on the other side of the world if they were small and light enough, toss them into the air like birds and then shoot them before their parents' eyes. Under fifty-two pounds? Exactly, my father says. *Lullaby and.* But stunts like that do absolutely nothing to advance the cause, my father says, because afterward the parents are even less likely to talk. I think we've reached the snow line. No, not at all, my father says, there are no limits to the imagination, even here, but after all our objective is to bring the truth to light. I, for example, was against sending your wet-nurse her daughter's hands, but in the end that was still better than arresting the wet-nurse herself. Don't you agree? Probably, I say. Better to give a warning first, to let her know where things stood. Yes, I say. And after all it did work, my father says, the wet-nurse finally left you in peace, and yet she herself is still alive as far as I know. Yes, I say, we ran into her not long ago. There, you see, my father says. A healthy dose of fear never hurts, he says. Adrenaline, he says, is produced by Mother Nature when a person is afraid, to heighten one's awareness of things that can help one. That sounds nice, I say. What? my father asks. Mother Nature, I say. Precisely, my father says. It's just as I always thought: The windows of the palace in which my father keeps everything in order, sirens wailing, are just painted on, not a single ray of sunlight ever enters the building, wailing and flashing, and these rooms devoid of light are filled with the struggle between justice, truth and love. The sirens have been transformed into birds and have flown out of sight. My father has bushy eyebrows which, in contrast to the blond hair that grows on his head, are completely black. When he smiles, he always furrows his eyebrows at the same time, making him look simultaneously cheerful and concerned. Now that I understand what things are like in Paradise, I am happy that my father is so often on duty. Now I know I have no reason to fear for him. If you aren't for us, you're against us, my father says, and this corresponds to the words that shoot through my head just before my eyes fall shut, his thoughts tuck my thoughts in tightly, and with his lips, which are as soft as those of a woman, my father gives me a goodnight kiss. I fall asleep. From now on, sleeping is my job.

The only light flickering in one of the lounges for the palace staff comes from the television. The announcer curses, wishes, prays and bellows. The men see and hear. When a long shot of the north curve fills the screen, it casts its pale reflection on their faces where they sit smoking, hissing through their teeth when their favorite lags behind. On the straightaway, the race cars can be seen close up for a few tenths of a second, darker and more vivid. At the lower edge of the screen you can read who is driving, how fast, in which position and so forth. The men seated before the television have their backs turned to the part of the room that lies in shadow, where a few beings trussed up like packages are lying on the floor with hoods over their heads—essence deliquescence—waiting for the truth to.

One really has to drag the words out of you. Just a simple hook will work as well. Even a clothes hanger if that's all you've got on hand. I'm trying to remember whom or what we turned our backs on when we lined up for assembly. The school building occupied the only edge of the quadrangle where no one was turning their backs on anyone or anything, closing off this edge of the square, but on the three other sides where we were standing, everything was open, and so every-thing that existed lay at our backs, we were turning our backs on everything that existed as we followed the advancing color guard with our eyes, just as we'd been instructed.

And now, my father says, the question is what to do with the material. Case A, if it's still alive, he says. House. Home. Go home. No no no, my father says, for us there's no going back, only forward. Just as in Nature, my father says. Off to distant shores. That's my father my mother up there flying to Rome to Rimini to Hawaii. There was always a doctor in atten-dance, he says. And a chaplain, of course. We released them into Heaven, still sleeping, my father says, and the chaplain prayed for them before their bodies hit the water. *The cradle will rock*. A miracle, far distant, the angels plummeting from blue to blue, from high up in the sky to the sea, sleeping, plunging, and still holding hands; my mother and I are standing down below at the harbor observing this miracle, and many other people are standing there as well, pointing at the angels and crossing themselves. Naturally, my father says, you have to take into account that the warm water on the ocean's surface displays a quite different pattern of currents than the cold water at the bottom. Pick the wrong spot, and the material will fail to sink but instead will get washed up somewhere at the feet of some beachgoer, and that's utterly unnecessary. Utterly unnecessary. The Arctic and Antarctic water masses, which are heavy because of their low temperature, sink to the bottom, my father says, when they collide with warmer currents, and in this way, flowing at enormous depths, they can reach all the way to the equator. All the way to the equator. Precisely, my father says. My father knows all about currents. But in order to take advantage of this effect, the flotsam must be cast overboard above the plateau of the ocean canyon situated at a depth of nine hundred and in parts up to one thousand three hundred meters below sea level. *Mirror mirror.* If, on the other hand, one discards something above the continental shelf, too close to the coastline, my father says, the warmer currents will cause it to drift along the shore, and it might well put down roots again a few towns away. And that is utterly unnecessary. No, I say, utterly unnecessary. When my father smiles, he draws up only one corner of his mouth, he entrusts one part of his face to the warmer currents. *The cradle will fall. When the bough breaks, the cradle will fall.* Then I smile as well. Then my eyelids fall shut.

I never would have thought there'd be so much music playing at the palace. From the outside, the building seems so quiet. Silence is health. Inside, though, people are ripping out other people's fingernails, you bitch, thwack, wham wham wham, *love is thicker than water, dance, stayin' alive*, and thwack, he's screaming his throat out, uh-huh, *stayin' alive*, and thwack, *night-fever, baby come back, with a little luck*, into the cesspool with you, thwack, *too much too little too late, the race is on, I can't let you go, and over again*, are you seeing stars yet, *love me please, just a little bit harder, I can still feel the glow*, heat, cold and wet, *I can't let you go*, give it to him, *and when you walk away from me baby, you're gonna be sorry*, you bitch, *together we can make it*, thwack thwack thwack, *no one knows who she is or what her name is, come on*, let's carve a flower in her right breast, in the left, in both, *let's go*, tell me what you see when you look on the dark side, *dance dance dance, so young to be loose and on her own*, tie her up by the hair, *hot child in the city, baby come back*, is black even a color, long live, *let's go, just a little bit harder*, put her on an iron bed, you, *you don't bring me flowers, you don't sing me love songs, you hardly talk to me anymore, when you come through the door at the end of the day*, a needle in the flesh, right next to the heart, it'll keep wobbling as long as it's still beating, a divining rod for the blood, a drum kit, drum it into him, beating, beating as long as the heart is still beating, *when I get home babe, I'm gonna light your fire, gonna wrap my arms around you, hold you close to me*, thwack, *I wanna taste your lips, I wanna kiss you all over*, shards of glass in your cunt, you old sow, *all over, till the night closes in, dance dance dance, it's easy to see when something's right and something wrong*, wham wham wham, thwack, wham wham wham, thwack, instruments made of metal in 4/4 or 3/4 time, it doesn't matter, just so it's louder than he is or she is, *love is thicker than water*, soften him up, him or her, with heat, cold and wet, bring her flesh to the melting point, then we'll see what's at the core, and then crack it between your teeth, crush it, grind it to dust, *stay with me, here with me, near with me, you're my one desire, dance dance dance, I need you babe, shadow dancing, three times a lady*, thwack, *follow me*, you bitch, *thicker than water*.

It all depends, my father says. For those who are already beyond sleep, Case B, there's always the classical variant, six feet under. Classic. With or without a stone. N.N. No Nonsense. No Needs. No Nothing. Nothing New. Nothing Natural. No Name, my father says. *In nomine patris*. What's your name, where do you live. So-and-so. One-A, Such-and-such Street. All just a matter of convention. Names, after all, are made by human beings and not the other way around. Of course, you can also sort according to the size and type of bones. The pits are then of corresponding size. But all in all it's easiest. And if there's no soccer field nearby, then just use a barrel filled with concrete, or else the foundation of some building. This too is a contribution to the development of our society, my father says, and looks simultaneously cheerful and concerned. Yes, I say. You were lucky that you were already here, my father says. And that I was on duty. Father. Mother. Ball. Car. From the very first moment I saw you, he says to me, I loved you. Lucky. If a person couldn't care less about children, then it doesn't matter to him, just so a mother with her baby or a woman far along in her pregnancy will still fit into a barrel. But children are our future. Lucky. I always knew that. And the future belongs to us, he says. That which is wrong will not survive. What is sick will die out, he says, just as in Nature. But the future belongs to us, my father says. And the future is our children. That which is wrong will not survive. What is sick will die out. But the future belongs to us.

Dumb man in the mountain, dumb child on his arm | Dumb the moun-tain, dumb the child: | Holy dumb man, bless this wound. To staunch the blood.

You needn't worry about the woman who gave birth to you, my father says. Her head was full of shit. That's a filthy word. And with all the other shit in her head, my father says, she forgot she had a child. Lucky lucky. A person who knows the laws and refuses to abide by them, my father says, has only himself to blame. And concrete, he says, is almost like amber, lucky, anything inside it will be preserved forever, forever, it's just that it isn't transparent, the concrete, and you don't hang it around your neck because it's too heavy. One corner of my father's mouth is being blown towards the equator.

I can remember the breasts of my wet-nurse quite clearly.
I drank from them a long time.
Silence.

Your father had already been processed. Though at the time I didn't know he was your father. Just a trick of chance. Just the way chance sits in its iron chamber, making calculations. A person who is sleeping, by the way, falls more quickly. Sleep makes the body heavy. It's really true, he says. Funny, isn't it.

Our Father. Creator of Heaven and Earth, who, moved by your infinite fatherly love, have spoken to us through your own son Jesuschrist to show us the way to true happiness through your Gospel; your son who died on the cross out of love for us took our sins upon himself and showed us that all our sufferings hold within them the truth of salvation; and with his resurrection from the dead he gave us the certainty that one day all departed believers will rise up once more, Father, we who remember the departed Correa beseech you, grant us the presence of the Holy Spirit and favor us with your love, which looks so kindly upon us.

In return we promise to live day after day like good Christians, we shall uphold God's commandments, aid our brothers and love them with the same generosity and faithfulness as our unforgotten departed Correa, in whom we have recognized the true meaning of Christianity.

For this we beseech you in the name of Christ our Lord.

From the very first moment I loved you, he says, and strokes my hair. Nothing is inherited, my father says. *Bone to bone, blood to blood*. That's all ridiculous. The way a child thinks is purely and solely a question of upbringing. Sorting. *Limb to limbs*. Your innocence, my father says. Have a look, says the young woman who has stepped from the garden into the room and is showing me her arm, on the inside of her elbow I see a small oval mole. I hold out my arm. On the inside of my elbow I see a small oval mole. You hadn't yet learned anything that was wrong, says my father, on whose lap I am still sitting, you were absolutely pure. Sorting. Three or four words perhaps. But beyond that, nothing. I could see it in your eyes, he says. That is why I loved you, says my father, from the very first moment. A child is given birth to by a mother, but is not part of that mother, praise God, he says. You were still free. Sorting. Father. Mother. Ball. Car. Through the young woman, I see the half-open door, and behind it flowers and weeds. And behind the flowers and weeds, the sea. Praise God. *Thus be they bonded.*

The young man is calling me, he wants to play ball with me in the depths of the sea, among the schools of fish and mussels. Let's go, I say. But just as he is about to shoot the ball to me, his shinbone is caught in a current and goes swaying off, and when he tries to catch the ball with his hands, one of his hands gets caught in the algae, and while the other one touches the ball, it cannot grasp it because the little bones, each of them separately, are floating free, it is the missing flesh prevent-ing the ball from being caught. The young man smiles at me, now it's my turn, I give the ball, which has slowly floated toward me all on its own, a push in his direction, the ball lands gently in the middle of the man's smile, it knocks the jawbones away from one another and lightly separates the upper jaw from the roof of the skull in which the imprints of veins can still be seen like a flower pattern, and so in the end it separates the smile from the smile.

When they find us, I am still sitting on my father's lap. At some point I fell asleep. On the lap of my father. They came in from the garden, or from the sea, to pluck me away from him, but that doesn't work, at first they just circle about, tugging at us, but in the end they realize they'll need a knife to separate us one from the other, and so they cut our arms through where they appear to have grown together, funny, isn't it? Now my and my father's tendons, muscles and all the blood are just lying there exposed. Everything is just as my father said it would be: They want to separate us one from the other and then take possession of your blood, he said, they want to pour your blood, doesn't one say spill, that may well be, or perhaps just drink it straight down, he said, but if they try to separate us, in the end all they'll have in their possession is at most the air that was between us, and the air isn't worth much, is it now? Nonetheless, my father says, or perhaps my blood will then flow like a rivulet through the separation, spill it and then something will grow, I've no idea, my father said, or else he said nothing at all, I think I've gotten things confused, my father merely held me on his lap a long time, a very long time, until finally I fell asleep in his arms, and he didn't say anything else, just sat there in silence.

It is written in my blood, they say, that my father is not my father, my mother not my mother and so on. The wood of the railing on which I keep a tight grip has such a beautiful dark gleam to it. Polished by the many hands that have already gripped it. I know, I say. With ninety-nine point five percent certainty. I know, I say. My father and my mother are standing trial here because when my father and mother, my father and mother, my father and mother... And then seized possession of me. Seized. I know, I say, of course. My father already told me everything. My name isn't. Yes. And my birthday presents too were on the wrong day year after year. Certainly. Certainly. On the table with wheels. *Plume in the summer wind, waywardly swaying.* But some day of the year is bound to be the day on which I was born, some day of the year is bound to be my birthday. Of all the many days of the year, some day that was there all along. Some word of all the words will no doubt be the last word some day, knife perhaps, or some other word, some word that was there all along. They show me photographs. The young woman. The young man. *Thus be they bonded.* Now I've been liberated, they tell me. That's good, I say. Liberated from Grandmother, who drinks in the morning, from the widowed aunt in a region of the country where snow sometimes falls, from the uncle who was struck by a car, from Grandfather through whose hands properties circulate, from Grandmother number two, who speaks two different languages, from woolen cap with pompom, wooden floor in which the door of my room scrapes a semicircle when it opens, from pink-colored house, smell of tobacco, Rose of Jericho, the dew in the garden, the salute to the flag and so on. Now I've been liberated from virtually everything. At the very bottom of the wooden toy chest lie a few crumbs, a rusted key ring and a broken crayon. Now they ask what I want to do now, now that my father and mother will have to go to prison and my father and my mother have been dead so many years. Sleep, I say.

Don't talk with dirt in your mouth, she says to the young man and the young woman. She takes care of the house. She waits. When she visits her father in prison, he says: Don't forget, the future belongs to us. It's true that the ones made of stone have been toppled from their pedestals and carted away, but their roots continue to branch beneath the entire city. Just wait, it'll pass, her father says. They have no idea how to extermi-nate their enemies. Dilettantes, he says. Yes, she replies.

And to think I even paid her, her father says, and spits on the tile floor at his feet. He always repeats this sentence, spitting each time as well, when the topic of the housekeeper comes up, ever since the words natural born were used in court in connection with this woman. When she now walks past the palace in which until recently her father worked, she sees many of the people who walk past the building spitting as well. The only difference is that her father's spit is removed each day when his cell is cleaned, while the spit on the street before the palace in which her father used to work dries and leaves behind whitish marks, as if the spit contained a tiny bit of salt. You see, her father says, these days you can no longer trust anyone. No, she says. Since the visitors have stopped frequenting her room, there's no longer any need to serve refreshments.

Her father told her the truth, she says to Anna when she finds her standing at the door. Now she knows everything. Oh, Anna says. And, she says to Anna, she loves the truth. She loves the truth with all her heart, she says to Anna. And Anna, whose mother was an Indian and was trampled to death by horses but is currently on a cruise along with Anna's father, who was attacked by a rabid wolf but meanwhile is in the best of health again, while Anna's sister had herself shot dead out of love, besides which the volcano, the giant pike, and no one knows yet how much longer the cruise will last: Anna nods and says goodbye.

As you see, her father says to her, I could just as well be lying on the sofa at home reading. And it won't be much longer now. Definitely not, she says to him. There just aren't enough of them left. And the ones that are left still respect me, he says. She nods.

Now she always walks through the city all alone, and the city is as good as empty. The traffic lights are working, but there are very few cars on the road, and hardly any pedestrians at all. That's not surprising, her father says to her, they just laze around the house all day long, they have no idea what it means to work, they sleep late, then they take a break for lunch, and after that it's already time to stop for the evening. That's no way to build a state, her father says. Definitely not, she replies. The only person she regularly encounters on the street is the old woman with the many plastic bags puffed out with wind. She still walks rustling down the street, looking as if it wouldn't cost her even a smile's worth of effort to rise up in the air, that's why she always squanders a smile, just like at their first encounter, by tossing it backwards over her shoulder. The old woman was already old the first time she saw her in the company of her wet-nurse, and old she has remained. If a person were to try to prick a hole in one of her bags, he wouldn't improve matters but wouldn't make them any worse either.

What a difficult time they had toppling the men of stone from their pedestals, she says. Because although the stone was just sitting on top, all the innards were made of concrete from the bones to the kidneys, and the concrete was much harder than granite. They really struggled with it, she said. Good, her father says. Finally they were forced to cart off all the concrete parts in one piece. You see, her father says. I think I'm interested in the real estate business, she says. Selling earth with air on top of it. Good, her father says. That's something you can live on.

The market hall has reopened, but with only a few vendors. One day the cobbler's blinds were rolled up again, and the large machine was carted away. A hairdresser took over the shop with the shadowy interior smelling of machine oil and began to trim the hair of this or that client beneath the sign still reading 'Shoe Repair and Locksmith.' But most of the time he stood in the doorway waiting for customers. Meanwhile the shop has closed again, beneath the sign still reading 'Shoe Repair and Locksmith.' When the first railroad line was to resume service, all the nation's children were called on to pull up the grass growing between the tracks along the entire stretch. They were given points for every meter of track they weeded, and the girl who collected the most points was featured in the newspaper along with her squint. On its maiden voyage along this cleanly weeded stretch of track, the garland-adorned train hit a bomb and was blown up along with the conductor, crew and guests of honor. Hereupon the reintroduction of train travel was postponed. That's what I read, anyhow, her father says.

For the last few days he's been allowed to read the newspaper. Just imagine, he says.

The signature with which she confirmed that the house with all its furniture now belongs to her is a hybrid. The first name that her parents gave her at birth paired with her parents' last name. Her name is thus a meeting place for all sorts of different people, just like all the other words in the language or the money that passes through so many hands, some of which might some day have occasion to chop off others and put them in packages. House and furniture are intended to serve as compensation, she was told. For everything she'd been through. She sells only the piano. Her father's room still smells of tobacco, though it's been quite some time now since anyone has smoked there. He's even allowed to have tobacco now, her father says, it's just like a hotel. Just wait, he says, it won't be much longer now. No, she says, definitely not. Meanwhile she looks after the house and everything within it: the wardrobes, mirrors, highboys, chandeliers and gothic benches.

Outside, something or other is constantly being blown up these days: the arms, legs, bellies and heads of people waiting at bus stops or standing in line at some agency or simply out for a walk. Things can't go on like this much longer, her father says, you'll see, the country needs to be put back in order again.

The young man and the young woman now consist only of paper. From time to time they smile to themselves, always in the same way, in the one or the other newspaper. If a person has gone missing, the supply of pictures is quite naturally cut off at a certain point. The young woman who gave birth to her is already starting to look like her sister in these pictures, and the young man who fathered her appears to be her brother. Things might change, you never know. Some day the young woman who gave birth to her will look like her daughter, and the young man who fathered her like her son. She can use the newspaper to polish the windowpanes, or fold it into a little square to stick beneath a wobbly table leg, she can also, when she's cleaning vegetables, lay out the newspaper underneath and afterwards wrap the peels of the onions, carrots and potatoes in it and place the soft, round parcel in the trash.

When her father asks her on her visits, during which she is separated from him by a pane of glass, whether she doesn't want to visit her mother as well, she says: Uh-huh. Change is all very well and good, her father says. But eventually one needs to have a foundation to build on. Those who do the most criticizing, her father says, are the ones who don't want to work. It's easy to say what's wrong, her father says, if you aren't one of those who bear the responsibility. It's always easier to break things down than to build something up. A body consists primarily of hydro-carbons, her father says, and decomposes with the help of worms and woodlice when placed quite normally beneath the earth, but one might also, provided one has the technical knowledge, transform it into a diamond. Into something that will last. And that's a great deal more interesting, isn't it, her father asks. Yes, she says, it is.

Worms and woodlice.

After three years her mother comes home and goes back to frying fish, meat and vegetables in the kitchen in the evenings, washing lettuce, stirring and chopping, while she herself sits at the living room table drawing up contracts or talking on the telephone. In the newspapers in which her mother wraps up the peels after cleaning the vegetables, new, unknown faces are meanwhile smiling. Time marches on, her father says to her when she visits him in prison, as she does every Friday. Every Saturday morning she joins her mother in cleaning the house from top to bottom. Never again will a stranger cross my threshold, her mother declares. No, she replies. When her mother suggests to her that she finally come along to see the woman who knows what to do with hands, feet and faces to keep them looking young, she would like to see her mother fall down the stairs or out the window, or stab herself accidentally while slicing bread. Two years later, her father comes home as well.

The Book of Words:
Translator's Afterword by Susan Bernofsky

All books are transformed by their translations. Since in Jenny Erpenbeck's *The Book of Words* the transplantation from German to English obscures certain fundamental points about the story being told, I've decided to append a few comments to orient the reader. On its surface, the novel has nothing to do with Germany at all; it is set in a foreign country, apparently located in South America, that remains curiously undefined, as nameless as the little girl who is the book's protagonist. To be sure, a number of clues invite us to think of Argentina in particular as a model for this country: This is where Saint Difunta Correa is most commonly worshipped, and the novel's first two epigraphs come from an article on the victims of political purges during Argentina's "dirty war" (1976–1983). But the basic anonymity of Erpenbeck's setting is crucial: *The Book of Words* is no historical novel, it is a parable of life lived in a state of endless subtraction, with words, objects and people constantly being taken away. This is the most innocent possible perspective on life in a totalitarian society where freedoms are drastically limited, divergent opinions outlawed, and critics tortured and killed.

One of the many countries this parable might invite us to think of is the East Germany of Erpenbeck's childhood, where mysterious disappearances, interrogation and imprisonment were sometimes a part of life. Occasionally—such as when the girl's father uses the word "material" to refer to the corpses of torture victims—the book invokes the sort of bureaucratic language associated with the Stasi, the secret police of the German Democratic Republic, and the Socialist Unity Party that backed it. This co-opting of language to frightening political ends underlies the book's nostalgia for a time when the words just meant what they meant, when they were "stable, fixed in place" and "intact."

But the novel's "Germanness" comes out most clearly in all the German children's songs and nursery rhymes incorporated into it, some of them as unsettling as the tales of the Grimms. These include a traditional St. Martin's Day song; a rainy-day rhyme promising a sick child a swift return to health; a ditty about a little bird arriving with a letter from a child's mother; a ballad about washerwomen; lines from *The Magic Flute*; and a mealtime prayer. Also featured is a popular rhyme for bouncing a child on one's knee as if on horseback: *Hoppa, hoppa Reiter, | wenn er fällt, dann schreit er. | Fällt er in den Graben, | fressen ihn die Raben. | Fällt er in den Sumpf, | macht der Reiter plumps!* (Hippity-hop rider, if he falls he'll scream. If he falls in the ditch ravens will eat him. If he falls in the bog he'll go plop.) There are even a pair of magic spells that represent a deep stratum of German historical consciousness. The Second Merseburg Incantation quoted in the epigraph is a healing spell for broken bones (originally used on an injured horse); the manuscript dates from the ninth or tenth century, though the spell may be much older. The second spell quoted in the novel, its purpose to staunch a bleeding wound, is recorded in an eleventh-century manuscript. Not every song and rhyme quoted in the novel is German—the attentive reader may notice an aria from

Rigoletto as well as a 1978 hit list sampler—but most are, and their cultural specificity sticks out in a setting otherwise marked as South American.

While these rhymes, songs and spells have been translated (or in a few cases replaced with equivalents sharing similar resonances), remembering that they represent a cultural heritage of Germanness is important for the background story of Erpenbeck's novel. We are told several times that the girl's mother, whom the girl hates and fears, is an outsider in their country: she has "eyes the color of water," which she attempts to hide in church by keeping them cast down, and was born somewhere far away, in a place where there is snow. We see our young narrator puzzling over an old photograph of her mother as a baby wrapped up in blankets and lying on a sled, her cheeks flushed with the cold. The girl has never met her maternal grandfather, but when near the end of the book her father begins to talk to her about torture techniques he has used, he also reveals a particularly grisly bit of family history: "Your mother's father, your grandfather, whom you never met, used to toss children into the air on the other side of the world if they were small and light enough, toss them into the air like birds and then shoot them before their parents' eyes." This "other side of the world," we are invited to imagine, is Germany under National Socialist rule—yet another state with a legacy of torture, and one from which many a torturer fled after the second world war, finding refuge in South America. These German songs may really be, quite literally, part of this little girl's childhood. *The Book of Words*, its eternally sunshine-filled present tense notwithstanding, takes us back to Nuremberg, the Black Forest, and a bunker in Berlin.

For news about current and forthcoming titles
from Portobello Books and for a sense of purpose
visit the website **www.portobellobooks.com**

encouraging voices,
supporting writers,
challenging readers

Portobello
BOOKS